THE RENEGADE REPORTERS

THE RENEGADE REPORTERS

ELISSA BRENT WEISSMAN

Dial Books for Young Readers

Dial Books for Young Readers
An imprint of Penguin Random House LLC, New York

First published in the United States of America by Dial Books for Young Readers,
an imprint of Penguin Random House LLC, 2021

Copyright © 2021 by Elissa Brent Weissman

Visit us online at penguinrandomhouse.com.

Library of Congress Cataloging-in-Publication Data is available.

Printed in the United States of America

ISBN 9780593323038
Premium ISBN 9780593531983

10 9 8 7 6 5 4 3 2 1

Design by Cerise Steel
Text set in Gazette LT

For LuAnn, Tom, Chris, and Taryn

CHAPTER 1

THIS JUST IN:
More Fallout from Dancing Gym Teacher Incident

For Ash, watching *The News at Nine* from inside the control booth was like watching her little sister try to tie her shoes; Ash could do it so much better if she were only allowed to help. Once the broadcast went live, she wanted so desperately to jump in and take over that she had to press her feet together to keep them from carrying her into the studio.

"Good morning, John Dos Passos Elementary," said the lead anchor, Harry. He was staring straight into the camera with a smile so tight, he had to speak through stretched lips, like an amateur ventriloquist. "Today is Tuesday, September tenth. The cold lunch is turkey sandwich. The hot lunch is spiral rotini with tomato and sauce broccoli."

Ash raised her eyebrows.

Harry's co-anchor, Damion, nudged Harry with his elbow and whispered something.

Harry squinted at the cue cards, his forced smile still

set. "Today's hot lunch is spiral rotini with tomato and broccoli sauce."

Damion looked at Harry and shook his head. The cue card holder took a step closer, which meant her back now blocked the camera.

"Tomato sauce and broccoli!" Harry said triumphantly, though viewers could see nothing but the cue card holder's hair.

"Camera one, you're blocked," Brielle, the director, said into her headset.

If Ash's best friend, Maya, had been operating camera one, she'd have known just what to do. "Pan right slowly," Maya whispered, as if to prove the point. But no one could hear her, because she was in the control booth with Ash. Khalil was lead cameraman now, and he didn't pan right slowly. Instead, he said "Yo," and pulled on one of the cue card holder's braids. She whipped her head around and glared at him—and at the whole school, since the camera was now capturing a close-up of her face.

Maya covered her eyes. Ash closed hers. She could hear laughs from classrooms down the hall. *The News at Nine* was broadcast live, which meant the whole school was witnessing this disaster.

"Ready camera two," said Brielle, cool as always. "Birthdays in three . . . two . . . one . . ."

The second camera operator was ready, but the birthday reporter wasn't. Now the broadcast showed him pulling at a thread on the bottom of his uniform shirt. It was one of those threads that just kept going and going, which meant he could have pulled it all morning if Damion hadn't shouted "Over to birthdays!"

The birthday reporter looked up, startled. "Birthdays," he said. "That's me." He dropped the thread and blinked at the camera. "Wait. Did you already do the Pledge of Allegiance?"

Ash shook her head. They'd skipped the Pledge of Allegiance. Sure, this was the first episode of the new school year, but this was basic stuff.

Director Brielle said, "Pledge of Allegiance in three . . . two . . ."

Right on cue, the editor in the booth cut to the video of a waving flag. But the birthday reporter, unaware, had decided he was finally ready to report the birthdays. "Happy birthday to kindergartener Curtis Thompson and third grader Madison—oh? We're doing the Pledge of Allegiance? Okay."

Damion said, "Please rise for the Pledge of Allegiance," but the editor in the booth now swapped the pledge screen for camera two, where the birthday reporter had resumed pulling the thread on his shirt.

The laughter from down the hall got louder, and Ash pressed her palms into her face. This broadcast was going off the rails. She was glad that she and Maya weren't part of it. Then again, if they *could be* part of it—more than having written the environmental report that Harry was surely going to butcher—Ash never would have messed up the lunch menu, and Maya never would have screwed up the camerawork, which meant *The News at Nine* never would have gotten off track in the first place. Ms. Sullivan was probably rethinking Ash and Maya's punishment this very moment, for the good of the show and the school's reputation.

Ash glanced over, and sure enough, Ms. Sullivan was biting her fingernails so intensely she could draw blood. It made Ash think of a word her babysitter had taught her: *Schadenfreude*. It was German, and it meant "taking pleasure in someone else's pain." Ash knew it wasn't nice to want the show to fail, but it was still sort of gratifying to see just how badly it was going without her and Maya.

"Brielle," Ms. Sullivan said. "Let's end the show early today. Cut to the closing credits."

"Ending the show early," Brielle said into her headset. "Closing credits in three . . . two . . ."

"I'm Damion Skinner," Damion said.

"And I'm Harry E. Levin," said Harry. "This has been *The News at Nine*, sponsored by Baltimore-based Van Ness Media."

The editor cut to the show's logo, a blocky number 9 with the words *The News at Nine* inside.

"Well," Ms. Sullivan said as the crew gathered in the

newsroom. "New year, new crew, lots to learn. But we'll get there."

Ash raised her hand. "Maybe we'd get there quicker if some of the old crew—I mean, some of the people with more experience—had bigger roles."

"*I'm* lead anchor, Ash," said Harry E. Levin. "Get over it."

"I was just speaking generally," Ash said.

"Yeah, right," said Damion with a snort.

Ms. Sullivan put out her hands like a referee. Then she took a long sip of her coffee, like she was going to need it if she was going to get through this day. If Ash drank coffee, she'd have done the same thing.

"Go ahead and get to class, everyone," Ms. Sullivan said. "Ashley, please stay and speak with me."

Maya shot her a worried look, but Ash shrugged. She was hopeful. Ms. Sullivan had seen how terrible the show was today without Ash in front of the camera or Maya behind it. She probably wanted to figure out a way to revoke their punishment and make Ash lead anchor without upsetting Harry. Ash planned to be very mature about it. Maybe she'd offer to share the role with Harry, alternating days or weeks. That would make Ms. Sullivan respect her even more, which might make her *insist* that Ash take over the role full-time.

Sure enough, once everyone had cleared out and Ms. Sullivan had gotten rid of Harry, who was zipping his backpack very slowly in an obvious attempt to eavesdrop, Ms. Sullivan leaned against a desk and smiled. "I know it's hard for you to watch *The News at Nine* from the booth, Ashley," she said. "You've been a dedicated member of the crew since—"

"Second grade," Ash finished for her.

Ms. Sullivan smiled again. "It must be difficult for you to watch Harry sit at the anchor desk instead of you."

Ash nodded. *Here comes the offer,* she thought.

"However," Ms. Sullivan said, "I'm not going to change my mind about your punishment."

Ash felt her face morph from hopeful anticipation to genuine shock. *What?*

"No matter how the show runs without you, we cannot have you back on-screen after what happened last year. And we can't have Maya operating a camera."

"I'm really sorry," Ash said for what must have been the five millionth time.

Besides, it wasn't even their fault. Well, not entirely. She and Maya had been roving reporters, walking to the gym to give a live status update on the new basketball hoop being installed. They'd heard a noise coming from the gym teacher's office and decided to investigate. Wasn't that what a good news reporter was supposed to do?

How were they supposed to know that Coach Kelly would be in there wearing nothing but shorts and a sports bra? How were they supposed to know that she wouldn't hear them coming because she'd also be wearing head-phones, dancing and lip-synching in the mirror while applying her makeup?

Okay, so Ash shouldn't have looked into the camera and said, "Breaking news: Coach Kelly's got moves!" She regret-ted that part of it (even though it *was* a compliment), and her first thousand or so apologies had been sincere. And maybe Maya could have shut off the camera quicker, but she *had* stopped recording the moment Coach Kelly turned around and screamed. That meant the 300 students and staff at John Dos Passos Elementary only saw about 5.4 seconds of the dancing gym teacher before *The News at Nine* cut to the sixth-grade anchors in the main studio. It definitely wasn't Ash's fault that the lead anchor was staring at the camera like a stunned raccoon, or that the co-anchor was laugh-ing so hard, a rubber band on his braces snapped. It wasn't Maya's fault that this made the lead videographer crack up and let his camera slip, which made it capture, sideways, the shock and hilarity that had engulfed the newsroom while a red-faced Ms. Sullivan frantically searched for the camera's off-button before the screen cut to black.

It wasn't Ash's or Maya's fault that *The News at Nine* was available to anyone with the password to the school's online portal. So, it also wasn't their fault that a former *News at Nine* reporter, now in high school, happened to watch this episode later that day, or that he'd decided to post the clip online for a wider audience. And it *certainly* wasn't Ash's or Maya's fault that the video racked up over two million views in just under five days.

Besides, Ash thought now as she pleaded silently with Ms. Sullivan here in the studio, all of this had happened in May—*last* year, before summer break—and Ms. Sullivan had taken them off the news crew for the rest of fifth grade. Surely that had been punishment enough. This was a new year, a fresh start. More importantly, this was *sixth grade*, Ash's last year at John Dos Passos Elementary and her only chance to be lead anchor for the morning news show. She'd been training for this opportunity since she was her little sister's age. Back then, her brown hair was still in long pigtails and her fingernails were unpainted and her top front teeth were just jagged lines poking unevenly through her gums. Now her hair was short and choppy, and her fingernails were purple and orange, and not only were her adult teeth fully in, but her face had finally grown enough to make them look the right size. In other words, Ashley Simon-Hockheimer had come a long way since she'd first joined the school news crew and had only been allowed to occasionally say "Who's there?" for the knock-knock joke of the week. She was a young woman now, an experienced journalist, and the most qualified person to be lead anchor, with her best friend, Maya Joshi-Zachariah, the undisputed choice for lead videographer. Together, they were an unstoppable team. An unstoppable team that was unfairly, devastatingly, permanently benched.

Ms. Sullivan took another long sip of her coffee. "We've been through this before, Ashley. You violated Coach Kelly's privacy. She was so uncomfortable, she moved to a different school. There need to be consequences."

Privacy, Ash thought, resisting the urge to roll her eyes, because what sort of privacy could you expect in a school full of kids? *If Coach Kelly really cared about privacy, she shouldn't have been dancing around her office in a sports bra.* "It won't happen again," Ash promised. "Trust me."

But Ms. Sullivan shook her head. "It's not just me who has to trust you. It's the principal, and the teachers, and the people at Van Ness Media who pay for all our equipment and sponsor the show."

"But won't the people at Van Ness Media be more embarrassed if the show is really bad?" Ash asked.

"Just because you're not lead anchor, it doesn't mean the show is bad."

"Today's show was really bad."

"Excuse me?" Ms. Sullivan said sharply.

"Nothing," Ash muttered.

Ms. Sullivan gave Ash a hard stare for a full five seconds. Then she said, "You're a strong reporter with a lot of experience. I know you care about broadcast journalism.

If you want to continue to write stories for the anchors to read, I'd love to have you be part of the crew. But you'll need to be a team player, which means you support the other members of the team no matter what. If you can't do that"—she crossed her arms—"I'm going to have to cut you from the crew entirely."

She said it gently but firmly, in that way teachers do, and Ash felt a sharp pang of betrayal. It was Ms. Sullivan who'd gotten Ash into reporting to begin with. Five years ago, she had substituted for Ash's first-grade teacher and asked for a volunteer to tell her what they were working on. Ash had stood up and given a complete rundown on what they were learning in every subject. Ms. Sullivan had been impressed. "You should consider joining *The News at Nine* crew next year," she'd said. "We could use a clear and confident reporter like you."

Ash still remembered how her six-year-old body had swelled with pride and possibility. She'd started watching *The News at Nine* closely every morning and dreaming about the day she'd be on the screen instead of watching it from her classroom. She'd signed up as soon as she was old enough, and she never looked back.

It was Ms. Sullivan who taught Ash about the importance of a free press and the responsibilities that came along with reporting the news. It was *The News at Nine* that taught Ash to investigate stories thoroughly and fairly, and to be confident and capable on camera and off. It was Ms. Sullivan and *The News at Nine* that had brought Ash together with Maya, who was too shy to speak around adults but silently noticed the things Ash didn't because Ash was too busy talking. Ash and Maya had been dedicated to *The News at Nine* for four years. How could Ms. Sullivan, of all people, do this to them, after just one little mistake?

Ash gulped, not wanting Ms. Sullivan to see her cry. It'd be hard to watch the show from her classroom, but as she knew from this first episode today, it'd be even harder to watch it from the control booth. She didn't think she could handle seeing Harry E. Levin read the things she'd researched and written, even if he did learn to do it without sounding like a robot. In fact, the better Harry delivered Ash's reports, the harder it'd be to watch.

Ms. Sullivan was right. There was no way Ash could be a supportive team player when she was aching to be captain. It'd be torture.

Ash swallowed, then squared her shoulders. "All right," she told Ms. Sullivan. "I quit."

CHAPTER 2

DEVELOPING STORY:
The Renegade Reporters

"You *quit*?" Brielle said at lunch.

"Yep," Ash said as she dipped a piece of spiral rotini into tomato sauce. "It was too hard to watch from the booth, especially with the show being such a disaster."

"Hey!" said Brielle.

"Oh my gosh, Brielle, no offense to you," Ash said. "You're an awesome director, and you did such a good job today, especially considering what you had to work with."

Brielle still gave her the side-eye, but Maya nodded vigorously as she finished a big sip of milk.

"You were like the captain on the *Titanic*," Ash said.

Brielle crossed her arms. "Steering the ship into an iceberg?"

"No," Maya said with a giggle. "Doing your best to avoid the iceberg, but it's just too big."

"The ship was sinking," Ash tried, "and you directed everyone into lifeboats."

"You saved the women and children," Maya added.

Brielle rolled her eyes behind her red glasses. "Okay, okay," she said. "No need to be extra."

Ash and Maya suppressed smiles. If anything was extra, it was Brielle's use of that word, which she'd picked up over the summer and had taken to saying constantly.

"Are you going to quit *The News* too, Maya?" Brielle asked.

"I don't know," Maya said. "I don't know what else I'd do after school."

Ash chewed on that along with her spiral rotini. *The News at Nine* crew met after school every Monday through Thursday to do their research and plan the next show. Maya's mom worked late, and Ash knew she wouldn't let her stay home alone all afternoon. Ash wasn't sure her own parents would let her do that either. She hadn't thought about that before quitting. She hoped her dads wouldn't make her join the after-school program, or worse, stay with her siblings and their babysitter, Olive.

"I don't really like writing reports, though," Maya said with a frown. "I'd rather operate the camera."

"I'd rather have you operate the camera too," Brielle said through bites of her turkey sandwich, "instead of Khalil. I need the show to be good if I'm going to get into the filmmaking program at Baltimore School for the Arts next year. And with Harry and Damion as anchor and co-anchor . . ." She trailed off, her head turning to the table where all three of those boys were sitting. "I mean, look at them."

Ash looked. They'd piled all of their sandwiches together to make an enormous bread-turkey-bread-turkey-bread tower, and now they were trying to see whose mouth was big enough to bite it.

"This should be one of our Games with Guests!" Damion said.

Ash felt like Damion had stabbed her with his plastic fork when he mentioned Games with Guests. It was a special *News at Nine* segment that aired every Friday in which teachers and other school staff competed in funny games.

"Damion, that's genius," said Harry. "Which teacher can eat a bigger sandwich?"

"We can keep adding layers and having them take bites," Damion said.

"Yeah!" said Khalil. He tried to take a bite of the monstrosity they'd made, but his mouth wasn't wide enough to fit the whole thing. The tower got squeezed into a triangle. Turkey, mayonnaise, and mustard came oozing out the side, dripping through Khalil's fingers and plopping onto the table.

As immature as the boys were, Ash thought their idea *would* make a funny Game with Guests. Hilarious even. And she knew her face betrayed it by the expression on Harry's when he happened to glance over at that exact moment. He gave a little smirk at Ash, then looked back at the boys. "The show is going to be so-o-o good this year," he said loudly. "Especially without a certain *roving reporter*."

Ash turned away, forcing back tears for the second

time that day. Harry E. Levin thought he was so cool, with his shark-tooth necklace and his ability to speak Chinese and his name that told his age. (So what? Ash's name was cooler, since *A.S.H.* were also her initials, and that would be true her whole life, not just the year she was eleven.) But Harry was a good student and a good drummer and the best maze-drawer in all of sixth grade. What if he was right, and he ended up being the best news anchor too? Maybe Harry and Khalil would do a better job than she and Maya ever could have done, and Ms. Sullivan would create a special award for them, and the sponsors at Van Ness Media would be so impressed, they'd decide to sponsor a new TV show called, like, *Live at Eleven with Harry E. Levin.* What if *Live at Eleven with Harry E. Levin* got picked up nationally, by a real television network? And Ash would be stuck at home with her little sister and her baby brother and their babysitter, watching her classmates deliver breaking news while her own newscasting dreams shriveled up and died. What then?

"Don't listen to them, Ash," Maya said.

"Yeah," said Brielle. "The three of us could make a better news show in my basement."

Ash chuckled. That was a funny thought. She picked up her fork and held it like a microphone. "I'm Ashley Simon-Hockheimer, broadcasting live from Brielle Diamond's basement, where you can see that her school uniforms are being washed as we speak."

"Laundry report in three . . ." said Brielle, "two . . . one."

Maya picked up her lunchbox and held it like a camera.

"We're currently in the spin cycle," Ash reported, "with the final rinse ahead. But if you'll follow me over to these storage shelves, you can see that the Diamond family is running dangerously low on toilet paper."

Brielle snorted and said, "Cut to commercial."

Ash grinned. "After the break, I'll interview Brielle Diamond herself about the shockingly low toilet paper supply. Stay with us."

Maya pressed an imaginary button on her lunchbox camera, then put it down on the table. "See? If I had a camera, we could totally record our own show."

"Except no one wants to watch a report about a washing machine," Ash said.

"Obviously," said Brielle, opening a bag of baby carrots. "We'd have to do real stories. Real news. Want one?"

Ash took a carrot and chewed it thoughtfully. She and her friends had four years' experience working on a news show. Between the three of them, they knew how to do in-depth research and make professional-quality recordings. They didn't have fancy Van Ness Media cameras and microphones, but did that really matter? Kids got famous online with far less. Come to think of it, Ash was *already* famous online—the dancing gym teacher video had millions of views—so they'd have that going for them too.

"What if we *did* do our own show at home?" she said slowly.

"Is that allowed?" Maya asked.

Ash gave a slow shrug. "Why not? Ms. Sullivan and Van Ness Media can't control what we do on our own."

"There's no chance they'd air it here at school, though," Brielle pointed out.

"They wouldn't have to," Ash said. "We could just put it online ourselves."

"But who cares about school news outside of John Dos Passos?" Maya asked.

"No one," Ash granted. "That's why we'd do other stories, like Brielle said." The idea was coming together as she spoke, spiraling outward and taking shape like a ball of cotton candy. It was just as sweet too. "Think about it. If it's not an official Dos Passos activity, we wouldn't have to stick to reports about school. We could report on anything, anywhere."

"Anywhere?" Maya asked nervously.

"Well, anywhere we're allowed to go alone."

"My granddad might come with us other places," Brielle said coolly. "He's around after school."

"Or my babysitter," Ash added.

"What about a camera?" Maya asked.

"You can use the camera on my phone."

"The quality won't be nearly as good," Maya said, but

her tone suggested that she was coming around to the idea. "Especially the sound."

"Yeah," Brielle agreed. "The footage will be rough."

"But it'll be real," Ash said. "Raw. That can be our image. Forget about roving reporters, we'd be *rebel* reporters—renegades!" She was getting excited now. She didn't need *The News at Nine* or even a sponsor like Van Ness Media to keep reporting the news. She had the best camerawoman and director in Baltimore City and an unlimited number of afternoons with nothing to do (except homework). "Picture it," she said. She put on her newscaster voice. "Remember the renegade reporters who recorded the Dancing Gym Teacher? They got kicked off their elementary school news crew, but that didn't stop them. Now they're back, hitting the streets of Baltimore, and they're reporting on much more than birthdays and lunch menus."

"The Renegade Reporters," Brielle said, nodding. "It's got a ring to it."

Maya gave a little squeal. "It'd kind of be like we're underground."

"Literally," said Brielle, "if our studio's in a basement."

Ash inhaled sharply, almost choking on her last bite of rotini. "Yes," she said once she'd swallowed. "Yes, that's it." She cleared her throat, picked up her fork, and held it to her mouth. "We're the Renegade Reporters, and you're watching *The Underground News*."

CHAPTER 3

Underground News Under Negotiation

Two days, three phone calls, and countless text messages later, *The Underground News* was still under negotiation. Maya's mom didn't want her unsupervised after school. Brielle didn't want to quit *The News at Nine,* and her parents worried that doing two shows would affect her schoolwork. Ash's parents didn't want her posting videos of herself online for the whole world to see. But the Renegade Reporters weren't the type to give up. They drafted a formal proposal, which Ash typed up in Van Ness Writer and handed to her dads during dinner on Friday night.

"Are you going to become a YouTube celebrity?" her sister, Sadie, asked.

"If by 'YouTube celebrity' you mean 'modern, self-made broadcast journalist,'" Ash said, "then yes."

Sadie giggled. "That sounds like 'spin,' right, Dad?"

"Expert spin," Mr. Simon agreed. "The question is, is it all spin and no substance?"

Ash crossed her fingers while he read the proposal. Dad

was a structural engineer, so it was his job to make sure new buildings were safely constructed, and he approached being a dad in much the same way. When it came to homework or chores or YouTube news show proposals, Ash knew Dad would ignore all the fancy distractions and make sure the foundation was solid.

"What do *you* think, Abba?" Sadie asked their other dad.

"I'm impressed," Mr. Hockheimer replied, buttering a piece of challah. "They've really thought things through. Except for the lighting." Abba was the lighting designer for a local theater, so it was no surprise that he'd zeroed in on their choice of studio. "Why on earth would you want to film in a basement?" he asked Ash.

"For the name," Ash explained. *"The Underground News."*

"It's a really good name," Sadie said.

"It is," Dad agreed. "And filming it in the basement won't give away our address or show too much of our home. I like that."

"Privacy is important," Abba agreed.

"More," said Beckett, kicking his legs and pointing a chubby finger toward the challah. Ash ripped a piece off her slice of bread and placed it on the tray of his high chair. Beckett clapped and stuffed it into his mouth.

"If Maya and I can record from our basement," Ash

continued, "we'll have adult supervision because Olive will be here watching Sadie and Beck. Brielle will do *The News at Nine* after school but work on our show on Fridays and weekends. She can log into Van Ness Movie Maker at home and edit the whole thing. Her parents said it's okay as long as she keeps her grades up, and it'll look really good on her BSA filmmaking application. And did you see item number seven? You guys get to watch and approve every episode before we post it."

"Yes, did you see that?" Abba said to Dad. "Us parents and guardians have twenty-four hours to view and approve each episode before it airs."

"Would you like more time?" Ash asked. "We can make it thirty-six hours, or even forty-eight. We can't go too long, though, or the news might be out-of-date."

"You know what you should report on?" Sadie said. "The big piles of dog poo all over the sidewalk."

"I don't think we need a report about that," Ash said. "Everyone in Federal Hill has already seen it. Or stepped in it."

"You should do a report on Baby Beck, then," Sadie said in a baby voice. "People will totally click on the ads if they have a cute baby."

Beckett squealed and kicked his pudgy legs, but Dad shook his head. "Baby Beckett is not going to be in any ads. Or on the show."

Ash inhaled. "Does that mean there *will* be a show?"

Her dads looked at each other. Ash looked at them. Sadie looked at Beckett. Beckett looked at his thumb. Finally, Dad and Abba looked at Ash.

"If it's okay with your friends' parents, it's okay with us," said Abba.

"Yes!" said Ash. She jumped up, ran around the table, and threw her arms around both of them.

"Thirty-six hours' approval time," Dad said from inside the group hug. "Nothing airs without our permission."

"Done!" said Ash.

"You girls need to stay with Olive."

"I promise," said Ash.

"Yes!" said Sadie.

"Yes!" said Beckett.

Yes! thought Ash. *Take that, Harry E. Levin.*

CHAPTER 4

Anchor and Videographer
Test Underground Studio

When school ended Monday, the Renegade Reporters did a triple fist-bump. Then Brielle headed to *The News at Nine* and the other two walked to Ash's house, carefully avoiding two piles of dog poo. "There was only one yesterday," Ash pointed out. "The dog poo bandit has been at it again. Sadie thinks we should report on it, but I don't think we want our first episode to be about dog poo."

"Definitely not," Maya said. "It's so gross. Why can't the owner just pick up after their dog?"

"Maybe it doesn't have an owner," Ash said.

"Like, it lives in a row house all alone?" Maya asked with a giggle.

Ash had meant that it was a stray, but now she pictured a dog standing on its hind legs and opening the door to its own house. She pretended to be a dog as she put the key in her lock and twisted it. They both barked and laughed as they entered, took off their shoes, and dropped their backpacks.

Like many row houses in Federal Hill, the Simon-Hockheimers' was over a hundred years old. It was long and narrow and had once contained many small rooms, but Dad and Abba had taken out most of the interior walls years ago, making the first floor one long, open rectangle with each room flowing into the next. It made the space feel open and airy despite its narrowness, but it also made privacy nonexistent. Standing at the front door, Ash could see straight through to the door at the back of the house. That also meant that everyone else—Sadie in the kitchen, Olive and Beckett at the dining room table—could see and hear her.

"I hear you two are mine every afternoon," said Olive, tapping her fingers together with faux wickedness. With Olive, though, it was a convincing faux wickedness. In addition to being a nanny, she was an actress. She usually did plays that were meant for grown-ups. ("It's avant-garde," Olive had told Ash about her last show. "You'd be bored to tears.") But she was currently rehearsing to be Puck in a production of *A Midsummer Night's Dream*, and she'd promised Ash and Maya front row tickets to the first Sunday matinee.

"We're your responsibility," Ash confirmed as she walked toward the dining room. "But it's not like you'll need to watch us. More like you'll need to keep Beckett and Sadie out of our way."

"Hey!" said Sadie, who stopped searching the pantry for a snack in order to put her hands on her hips.

"Yeah," said Olive. "That's no way to talk about your Story Scout."

"Is that what I am?" Sadie asked excitedly.

"Yep," Olive said. "It sounds fancy, doesn't it?"

"Fa-ee," repeated Beckett.

"Yes, very fancy," said Sadie.

"Too fancy," said Ash. "You haven't even given us a real story idea yet."

"*Yet*," said Olive with a wink.

"Ink!" said Beckett. He closed both his eyes tightly and then opened them again.

"Wink wink wink," said Olive. Back in nanny mode, she started tickling Beckett while making exaggerated winks, and he broke into baby laughs.

Spying an opening, Ash hurried down into the basement. Maya followed and closed the door behind her.

"Welcome to our new TV studio," Ash said.

Both girls fell silent, taking it in. Ash had never given much thought to her basement. It was just another part of her house. Until this moment, when she seemed to be seeing it for the first time, and through the eyes of Maya. But not her best friend Maya. That Maya had once spent a whole Saturday in this basement playing "holiday boutique," which meant she and Ash had taken turns "buying," "selling," and gift-wrapping everything in sight. That Maya had squeezed Ash's hand when Abba yelled at them for wasting three full rolls of wrapping paper, two dispensers' worth of Scotch tape, and the twenty minutes he had to spend unwrapping "presents" in order to find a tube of caulk to seal the toilet. That Maya didn't care one bit about the look of Ash's basement.

But at this moment, Ash was viewing her basement through the eyes of expert videographer Maya Joshi-Zachariah. Videographer Maya was used to working in *The News at Nine* studio, designed by Van Ness Media and filled with top-of-the-line broadcasting equipment. Ash's basement was only partially finished, so there were linoleum floors and brick walls and metal ducts running along the ceiling. Half of the basement was dug out, which meant both girls could stand upright without hitting their heads on a wooden beam or plastic pipe. But a set of two steps led to a section of the basement that was even less finished. That part had a concrete floor specked with dirt, and if one of the girls grew an inch—or wore her hair in a particularly high ponytail—she'd have to stand at a slant. Even Brielle, the shortest of the group, would have to avoid standing on tiptoe.

"It's not the *News at Nine* studio," Ash said apologetically.

And Maya, proving herself to be the best friend anyone could ask for, said, "Well, this isn't *The News at Nine*."

Ash felt the relief physically, like she'd just put down a

stack of heavy textbooks. Excitement restored, she asked, "Where do you think we should set up?"

Maya closed one eye, made her fingers into a box, and looked through it at one side of the room, then another. "We don't want too much stuff in the background," she said, "or people will be looking at the stuff instead of you."

"Good point."

"Maybe that wall over there? Let's do a test video."

Ash handed Maya her phone. Then she stood in front of the wall. "Tell me when to start."

"Anchor in three . . ." She stopped and shook her head, embarrassed. "I wish Brielle were here to do this part. Maybe we should wait till Friday when there's no *News at Nine* meeting, so she can be with us after school."

"It's only a test video," Ash assured Maya. "You don't need to be so official."

"All right." Maya still sounded unsure, but she held up Ash's phone and pressed record. Then she nodded and mouthed, "Go!"

"Test, test, test," Ash said in her news anchor voice. "This is the first test video from our new studio in my beautiful basement. Maybe we'll get some good footage for our blooper reel."

Outside, a city bus approached the corner. It let out a puff when it stopped, then made a heaving noise as it leaned toward the curb. With the basement windows right at ground level, the sound was so loud, it shook the room.

Maya wrinkled her nose and stopped recording. They watched the short take. It had picked up every decibel of the racket from outside. Not even Brielle's Van Ness Movie Maker skills could dampen that sound.

"Let's try someplace farther from the window," Maya suggested. "Maybe that corner by the steps?"

Ash went over to the corner, and Maya gave her the signal.

"Test number two!" Ash said loudly. "We're trying the corner, where a bus may still make the walls shake, but it might not destroy our ears."

They watched this new take. The sound was slightly better, but just as Abba had warned, the lighting was terrible. "My face is all shadowy." Ash sighed. "It's like I'm reporting from an open grave."

"Well, we said 'underground,'" Maya joked.

Ash grinned. "Live from the Greenmount Cemetery," she said, "this is *The Underground News*."

Maya held the phone up again and started recording. Ash grabbed a wrench from an open toolbox and held it up like a microphone.

"Tonight, we're going to meet with a very special guest," she said into the wrench, "Mr. Ebenezer Ebenezerus, who died in 1781. We'll ask him about changes he's seen in the cemetery over the past two hundred years."

Maya pressed her lips together in an effort not to laugh.

She motioned with her hand for Ash to keep going, and to move around as she spoke. So Ash walked slowly across the basement, keeping her wrench-microphone close.

"There's a full moon over the cemetery tonight, as you can see, so it's the perfect time to continue our ongoing series, 'Werewolves: Are They Real?'" Ash had now reached the place where the high ceiling ended and the low ceiling began. She lowered herself, slowly, onto one of the steps separating the linoleum floor from the concrete. "Later tonight, the Renegade Reporters will meet with Skeleton Sally, who'll show us how the ghosts plan to celebrate Halloween. Stay with us."

"Cut!" said Maya.

Both girls cracked up the second the camera was off.

"Skeleton Sally!" said Maya.

"Ebenezer . . . what did I call him?" Ash asked.

"Ebenezer Ebenezerus!"

When they'd calmed down, Maya said, "For real, though, Ash, I think this is the spot. Look how good it looks."

They played it back. It looked better than Ash could have hoped. Sun from the windows lit her face just right. The brick walls on either side were cast in shadow, but in a way that seemed artsy and hip. Sitting on the steps made Ash look casually cool, though still serious, like someone you'd want to meet for coffee between college classes. The concrete and even the dirt added to the whole effect. It was the exact opposite of the bright, polished, squeaky-clean *News at Nine* studio. In other words, it was exactly what *The Underground News* was going for.

"It's perfect," Ash said.

Maya squealed. "This is fun. Let's do one real take, just to get something down."

Their first episode was just going to be an introduction, something to ease the viewers in. The team had decided as much over the weekend, and they'd all agreed it was a good plan. But now that it was time to record it, Ash's stomach flip-flopped like she'd just done a loop de loop on a roller coaster. This wasn't a new sensation—she'd gotten it right before every news report she'd ever delivered—but it had been so long since she'd reported the news, she'd forgotten to expect it, and the surprise made her stomach do a second loop, right after the first. *You've got this*, the anchor told herself, the way she did every time the pre-show nerves made her body feel like an amusement park. But did she? It was one thing to read a teacher-approved script and have it transmitted to her elementary school. It was something else entirely to host her own YouTube show that could be viewed by anyone in the entire world.

"Remember," Maya said reassuringly, "we're not live. That means we can do as many takes as we want."

"You're right," Ash said slowly. Why hadn't she thought of that? That was why she and Maya made such a good team; Ash spoke for them both, but Maya was always in the background, helping her know what to say. Ash still felt like she might be on a roller coaster, but her shoulder harness was secure, because she was riding with Maya.

"You ready?" the videographer asked, her camera in position.

The lead anchor sat down on the steps. "Let's do this."

THE UNDERGROUND NEWS, EPISODE 1

REPORTER: Ashley Simon-Hockheimer
VIDEOGRAPHER: Maya Joshi-Zachariah
EDITOR: Brielle Diamond
SLUG: Intro

VIDEO	AUDIO
Anchor on Camera	**ANC**: Remember the dancing gym teacher? I never intended for that video to go viral. I also never intended for it to get me kicked off my school's television news crew. But that's what happened. My best friend was behind the camera at the time, and she got kicked off too.
	Just because we can't report the news at school, though, it doesn't mean we can't report the news. Together with our friend Brielle, the best video editor you'll ever meet, we decided to keep doing what we love and bring it straight to you—yes, YOU—whoever and wherever you are. So, subscribe to this channel for important, real, breaking news brought to you by the sharpest sixth-grade journalists in Baltimore City.
	I'm Ashley Simon-Hockheimer, we're the Renegade Reporters, and you're watching *The Underground News*.

CHAPTER 5

OPINION:
Nostrils Are Ugliest Part of the Face

The sixth graders were in art class creating self-portraits on tablets using Van Ness Art Studio when Harry E. Levin elbowed Ash in the arm.

"Hey!" she said. "I was drawing my nose. Now it looks like I have one giant nostril."

Harry studied her portrait's nose, then her real one. "It looks pretty accurate to me."

Ash clenched her teeth.

"Your mouth needs some work, though," he said. "It's way too happy in your picture."

"You drew *your* mouth closed," Ash retorted, "which it never is in real life."

"Harry. Ashley," said their art teacher, Mr. G. "Less talking, more drawing."

Harry tapped the screen to select a black crayon and started using his finger to draw his spiky hair. "I was going to tell you something important," he said, his eyes on his tablet. "But I guess I won't now, since you want me to keep my mouth shut."

"Yeah, right," Ash said.

"Uh-huh," Harry said. "For real. But now you'll never know."

Ash finished erasing her nose and crossed her arms. Becoming lead anchor had really made Harry insufferable. "Please tell me," she said.

Harry kept quiet.

"Okay, fine," Ash said. "I don't care. You probably didn't have anything to say in the first place."

"Did too."

"Harry," Mr. G warned.

Ash tried to focus on her nostrils. How were you supposed to draw nostrils, anyway? There was no way to do it that would make them look attractive, or even natural. She'd never given nostrils much thought before, but now that she did, she decided they were the ugliest part of the face.

"I *was* going to tell you that your sister's in the hallway," Harry whispered. "She was trying to get your attention. But I won't bother now because she's gone."

Ash looked at the doorway. No one was there. Leave it to Harry E. Levin to tell her someone was looking for her only after that person had left. She raised her hand anyway.

"Yes, Ashley?"

"Can I go to the bathroom?"

Mr. G sighed. "Take the pass."

Ash logged out of her Van Ness Media account so Harry couldn't mess up her portrait while she was gone. Then she took the bathroom pass and walked as quickly as she could out of the art room. She rounded the corner and saw two girls starting down the stairs at the far end of the hall. Ash recognized one of their backs. "Sadie!" she whisper-called. Not wanting to get caught running, she race-walked to the staircase. "Sadie!" she said again.

Both girls turned around. "Finally!" Sadie said. "I was trying to get your attention forever."

"Sorry," Ash said. "I was sitting next to Harry and he was being . . . difficult. What's going on?"

Sadie's face lit up, and she skipped back to the top of the steps. "I found news for you to report. Lucy's bike was stolen from Riverside Park yesterday."

"Whoa," Ash said. "For real?"

"Believe it," said the girl hopping up the steps, who Ash realized must be Lucy. She was wearing zebra-print leggings under her khaki jumper and a headband with wire cat ears on top. "Someone took it right from the playground, inside the fence and everything."

Ash knew she shouldn't be happy about a stolen bike. But it was hard to not be excited about this break for *The Underground News*. Here was a real piece of news—actual, serious news—that the Renegade Reporters could report.

Even better, the story had happened to Lucy, who clearly had a big personality. If she was up for an interview, she'd make for a dynamic first guest.

"Can I ask you some questions after school," Ash said, "so I can make my report as thorough as possible? And would you be willing to be interviewed on air?"

"I did so many chores to earn that bike," Lucy replied. "I saved my allowance for *months*. I will do everything in my *power* to get it back."

Ash couldn't suppress her smile. "So that's a yes, then?"

"Believe it," Lucy said for the second time.

"And you'll report it on your show, Ash?" Sadie asked. "I already told Lucy all about *The Underground News*."

"For sure," Ash said. "Thanks for the tip, Sadie. You've earned your title."

"Ladies," said a teacher who'd appeared at the top of the staircase. "Where are you supposed to be?"

"In class," said Sadie.

"We're going there," said Lucy.

The teacher waited. The second graders turned and hurried down the steps. Ash mumbled an apology as she walked past the teacher and back to art. But she stopped after rounding the corner. Someone was hunched over the water fountain. Someone with dark, spiky hair.

"What are you doing here?" Ash asked. "Were you following me?"

Harry stood up and wiped his mouth with the back of his hand. "Not everything's about you, Ashley. Maybe I was thirsty."

Ash crossed her arms. "You just suddenly got thirsty the minute I left to talk to my sister?"

Harry crossed his arms. "I can get thirsty any time I want."

Ash wasn't buying it. "Were you spying on me? Did you hear my conversation?"

Harry shrugged. "It's a big hallway. The sound might have traveled. It's not like we're"—he raised one eyebrow—"*underground.*"

Before Ash could react, a teacher stepped out of a classroom and cleared his throat loudly. Luckily, it wasn't the same one who'd caught Ash by the steps, or she'd have really been in trouble. "Get to class, both of you," this teacher said, "or would you rather go to the principal's office?"

Harry hurried off to the art room, and Ash followed behind, glaring at the back of his sneaky, lying head. *Who cares if he was spying?* she tried to tell herself. In fact, she hoped he was. Because *The Underground News* was about to blow *The News at Nine* out of the water, and the sooner Harry realized it, the better.

CHAPTER 6

Squirrels Squirreling at Scene of Crime

"Dogs chasing Frisbees, kids frolicking, squirrels . . . squirreling. That's what this second grader was expecting when she rode her bike to Riverside Park yesterday afternoon."

"Cut," said Maya. She put down the camera. "Squirrels squirreling?"

Ash shrugged one shoulder. "I don't know. What would you say squirrels do?"

"Creep people out," Maya said, giving a passing squirrel the side-eye.

"Kids frolicking, squirrels creeping people out." Ash shook her head. "It doesn't really go."

"Neither does the first part," said Lucy, who was making her way across the monkey bars. "I mean, who says 'frolicking'?"

"No one says 'frolicking,'" quipped Sadie, who was hanging upside down. "It's unnatural."

Ash sighed. They'd come to Riverside Park to record footage at the scene of the crime. But it was hard to be anchorwoman when everyone and their mom had an opinion about what she should say. (Literally. All the kids at the park were weighing in, as were their moms.)

"The sound is terrible here," Maya said with a frown. "The phone is barely picking you up at all because of the wind and the little kids running around."

"Frolicking," said Lucy, which made Sadie giggle.

But not Ash. "Do you want me to report on your missing bike or not?" she asked.

"Yes."

"Let's just record Lucy's interview," Maya suggested. "We can do your parts in the studio or on voiceover, and Brielle can edit it together."

"Good thinking." Ash looked up at Lucy, who was now doing the monkey bars two at a time. "Let's go over to the fence where you parked your bike yesterday."

"Wait!" Maya shouted. Then she shrunk back, embarrassed, and talked quieter. "If Brielle's going to be editing anyway, let me get some footage of Lucy up there. For background shots."

That was all Lucy needed to hear. The second the camera was on her, she began breaking out all her tricks. She skipped bars, hung upside down, spun by two fingers, and traveled the whole circle in what had to be world-record-worthy time. Sadie cheered from the ground, Olive whooped from the bench, and baby Beckett clapped from his stroller.

Once Lucy dropped down, Maya filmed her walking to the place where her bike disappeared.

"Tell me what happened yesterday when you got to the park," Ash said.

Lucy launched into her story with even more energy and passion than she'd displayed in the stairwell. She spoke loudly enough for the camera to pick up her voice clearly—and for other families in the park to hear what was going on.

"You have to be careful with your stuff around here," one of the moms said. "My diaper bag was stolen from this park about a year ago. It had my phone in it too, but not my wallet or keys, thank goodness. I filed a police report, but they never found it."

Ash could hardly believe it—or her luck. "Can I ask you about it on camera?"

The mom paused. "What's this for? A school project?"

"It's not part of school," the anchor replied. "It's for a show we're making ourselves called *The Underground News.*"

The mom looked from Ash and Maya to Olive, who waved from the bench. Then she looked at her own toddler, who was picking up handfuls of mulch and carefully arranging them along the bottom of the slide. "All right," the mom said, getting excited. "I actually used to play 'news show' in my room when I was a kid. I'd report on what I saw out the window, and I'd interview my stuffed animals."

"Cool," Ash said. She hoped she sounded convincing, even though having a pretend news show in your room wasn't that cool. Not compared to having a real show that people could watch all over the world. "Now's your chance to be on a real show, online," she told her.

The mom fluffed her hair and smiled at the crew. "Is there food in my teeth?"

Lucy checked carefully before saying "You're good."

That interview took only three minutes to record, which was good because Olive said they had to leave in five. Sadie and Lucy spent the last two minutes on the swings while Maya got some slow pans of the park, in case they needed more background footage. When their time was up, they all walked Lucy to her house, which was in the opposite direction of Ash's. Then they had to drop off Maya at hers, which was also out of the way, and along the route the dog poo bandit (or independent, home-owning dog) must have walked that day. By the time the Simon-Hockheimer crew got home, the sky was getting dark. Beckett was fussy, Sadie was snippy, and Olive was barely holding it together.

"There you all are," said Dad, who was straining a pot of pasta. "Big news day?"

Ash's feet ached and her stomach groaned, but she'd never felt more energized. "Live, local, and late-breaking," she said. "Just wait till you see."

THE UNDERGROUND NEWS, EPISODE 2

REPORTER: Ashley Simon-Hockheimer

VIDEOGRAPHER: Maya Joshi-Zachariah

EDITOR: Brielle Diamond

STORY SCOUT: Sadie Simon-Hockheimer

SLUG; Stolen bike

VIDEO	AUDIO
Anchor on Camera	**ANC:** Coming up, breaking news on crime in South Baltimore. I'm Ashley Simon-Hockheimer with the Renegade Reporters, and this is *The Underground News.*
Intro and Credits	NONE
Anchor on Camera	**ANC:** This just in from John Dos Passos Elementary School. A second grader's bike was stolen from Riverside Park. *The Underground News* went to the scene of the crime.
Panorama of Riverside Park	**ANC voiceover:** Dogs running, kids playing, people out for a stroll or relaxing in the pavilion. That's what this seven-year-old was expecting when she rode her bike to the playground yesterday afternoon.

Lucy at Playground	**LUCY:** I came to the park with my aunt and my little cousins Tuesday afternoon at about four thirty. I rode my bike and parked it right here, inside the fence, by the playground. I went on the monkey bars, the swings, the climbing thing—you know, the usual stuff.
Lucy Hanging Upside Down on Monkey Bars	**ANC voiceover:** But it wasn't a usual day. Not by a long shot.
Lucy at Playground	**LUCY:** When we went to leave, my bike wasn't there. It was gone. My aunt and I looked everywhere. Someone must have taken it while I was playing.
Anchor with Neighborhood Mom at Playground	**NEIGHBORHOOD MOM:** I take my two-year-old to this park almost every afternoon. It's crazy that someone's bike was stolen from inside the fence, but I can't say I'm too surprised. **ANC:** Have you experienced crime at the playground yourself? **NEIGHBORHOOD MOM:** About a year ago, my diaper bag disappeared, right out of my stroller. It had my phone in it too. Ever since then, I make sure to keep all my valuables on me while my son plays.

Anchor on Camera	**ANC:** Theft may be a common problem, but that doesn't make it any easier for the victims.
Lucy at Park	**LUCY:** My bike didn't just come down from the sky, you know. And it wasn't like Santa gave it to me either. I did chores and saved my allowance to earn that bike, and some chump just took it when I wasn't looking. It's not fair.
Photo of Lucy on Her Bike	**LUCY:** My bike—I called it the Yellow Flash—is black with yellow flames on it. It had red, white, and blue ribbons through the spokes from the Fourth of July parade. And one of my handlebar grips was kind of ripped, but I could still hold it just fine.
Lucy at Park	**LUCY:** If you're watching this and you see the Yellow Flash somewhere, contact *The Underground News.* I'm offering a reward of ten pieces of my saved Easter candy, even the Snickers. And if you're watching this—yes, YOU, the THIEF who STOLE the Yellow Flash— now's the time for you to do the right thing and return what doesn't belong to you. What goes around comes around, and if you do bad things, bad things WILL happen to you. Believe it.
Anchor on Camera	**ANC:** I'm Ashley Simon-Hockheimer, and this has been *The Underground News.*

CHAPTER 7

Subscriber 27 Deemed Suspicious

The whole team recorded Ash's anchor spots on Friday afternoon. Maya drew them a logo on Saturday, and Brielle spent most of the weekend putting it all together in Van Ness Movie Maker. She posted the bike theft episode to YouTube on Sunday night at eight p.m., immediately after their grown-ups granted their contractually obligated approval.

Ash wrote up an email for her dads to send to all of her extended family. Maya and Brielle did the same. They shared the YouTube link with Lucy and her family, who were so pleased with her performance that they shared it with everyone they knew. Ash refreshed the screen on repeat until her dads dragged her from the computer and took away her phone. They allowed her one quick look before she went to bed at 9:35. The video was up to fifty-seven views, about twenty of which were probably by Ash herself. But in the morning before school, the count was up to eighty-five, and none of the extra twenty-eight could have been by Ash, because she'd been asleep! Even better, their channel had twelve subscribers, which meant twelve of the people who'd watched this episode wanted to see more, and the video had an ad at the bottom for "Local Baltimore news on WBAL," which Ash took as a high compliment.

On Monday after school, Ash showed the episode to Olive, who shared it with her many friends and followers, which meant by the time Ash brushed her teeth that night, the count had climbed to 140 views and twenty-six subscribers. And just as she said good night to her dads, her phone vibrated with an alert of their twenty-seventh subscriber: Someone with the account name thebestharry11.

Ash gasped. She clicked to view thebestharry11's profile, but Abba took the phone out of her hands. "Bedtime, Ashley," he said. "You know the rule."

"But—"

"Whatever it is, it will still be there tomorrow."

It was. And it was worse. Not only had Harry E. Levin watched Ash's show and subscribed to her channel, he was planning on stealing her story.

"Lucy's going to come on *The News at Nine* tomorrow," Brielle reported at lunch, "to talk about her stolen bike."

"What?" Maya said, nearly spilling her milk. "But how—"

"Harry. He brought it up this morning, right when we finished recording."

Ash stared at Harry's table, seething. So he *had* been

spying on her last week in the hallway. How else would he have found *The Underground News* or Lucy?

"Can you kill it?" Ash asked Brielle. "Like, as director of *The News at Nine*, say you don't think you should cover the story?"

Brielle chomped a baby carrot skeptically. "You know I don't really have that much power. And Ms. Sullivan was, like, really into the idea. She said it was a great lead."

"Of course it is," Ash said, squeezing her napkin into a ball. "Because it was *our* lead." It wasn't enough for Harry to steal her anchor role at *The News at Nine*, now he had to steal her story and her guest too? And there was nothing Ash could do about it. Confronting Harry wouldn't make one bit of difference; it would probably just egg him on. She could try to make Lucy change her mind about going on *The News at Nine*. But Ash had a feeling that Lucy wasn't the type to turn down any chance to be on TV, or the opportunity to make more people aware of her stolen bike.

"Our reporting will be better," Maya reasoned, "because we were able to shoot at the park. All Harry can do is ask Lucy questions in the studio."

"And he can't say he *broke* the story," Brielle added. "Because *we* reported it first."

"But it's not like he asked our permission," Ash grumbled, "or is going to give us credit for our hard work."

"I can try to make him do that, at least," Brielle said.

"Yeah," Maya said hopefully. "Ms. Sullivan was always serious about us citing our sources. It's the responsible thing to do."

A loud laugh came from where the boys were sitting. Khalil was squirting water out of his drink bottle across the table and into Damion's mouth. Damion held up his lunch tray as a shield. The water ricocheted off the tray and onto Harry, who pretended to be taking a shower.

The Renegade Reporters looked at one another and sighed. "Right," Ash said. "We just have to count on *those* boys to do the responsible thing."

CHAPTER 8

YELLOW FLASH OWNER:
"Believe It!"

"Good morning, John Dos Passos Elementary," Harry said. "Today is Wednesday, September eighteenth. The cold lunch is tuna salad and crackers. The hot lunch is black bean burrito bowl. I'm Harry E. Levin."

"I'm Damion Skinner," said Damion. "And you're watching . . ."

"*The News at Nine*," they said in unison. Well, sort of. Damion said "*The News at Nine*," at the same time Harry said "*News at Nine*," which meant they were off by a word, so Harry repeated "*Nine*" at the end to try and match Damion, only his timing was off, so Damion tried to match him, so it sounded something like "*The News News at at Nine-Ni-Ni-Nine?*"

At her desk in her classroom, Ash winced just a little bit. She usually tried to ignore her old show, but today she was dialed in completely. She knew Harry was going to steal her story—last night at dinner, Sadie had confirmed that

Lucy was planning to be on *The News at Nine,* along with a framed photo of the Yellow Flash. Dad and Abba spent most of the evening reminding an angry Ash that news wasn't limited to any one anchor or network, that television stations were always competing for viewers, that viewers tuned in not just for what was reported but also *how* it was reported. Ash thought all that was easy for her dads to say. They'd never had their ideas stolen from right under their noses.

The News at Nine proceeded as usual, with the Pledge of Allegiance, the birthday report, and, it being Wednesday, the knock-knock joke of the week. And then the anchors were back on screen, both grinning with anticipation, like they were about to jump from behind the desk for a surprise birthday party.

"And now," Harry said, "a special report about a second grader at our school."

Ash and Maya caught each other's eyes. Ash shrugged half-heartedly, and Maya frowned.

"Last week, Lucy Wilson's bicycle was stolen from the playground at Riverside Park," Harry said.

"Terrible," said Damion, shaking his head.

"Lucy rode the bike, which she called the Yellow Flash, to Riverside Park. She parked it inside the fence, near the playground. When she was done playing and ready to ride home, the bike was gone. Here's Lucy Wilson herself, with breaking news on this developing story."

Breaking news? Ash plopped her head into her hands, exasperated. She hadn't expected Harry to credit her reporting, even if Brielle had tried to make him. But calling his report "breaking news" was a flat-out lie. He couldn't call it that, not when Lucy was about to walk into the studio and repeat the facts from her interview with Ash.

But then Ash's head dropped out of her hands and almost onto her desk. Because Lucy didn't walk into the studio holding a photo of her stolen bike—she *rode* into the studio *on* her stolen bike.

"The Yellow Flash!" Lucy shouted. "It's back!"

The kids in Ash's classroom cheered and started talking excitedly. Ash and Maya exchanged confused looks. What was going on?

"How did you get the bike back?" Harry asked.

"Get this," Lucy said, parking the Yellow Flash next to the anchor desk but not getting off. "I went to Riverside Park last night, and my bike was *there*. Right in the exact spot it had been taken from."

"Did you see who brought it back?" Damion asked.

"Nope," Lucy said. "There were some people at the park, but they said the bike was there when they got there."

"And it's definitely yours?" Harry asked.

"Believe it!" Lucy pumped her fist in the air. "It's kind of beat-up, though. Both handlebar grips are ripped now, see? And I had ribbons in the spokes, which are gone. But it's definitely the Yellow Flash." She climbed down and gave the bike a big hug. She rested her head on the seat and said, "I missed you, Flashy. Don't ever leave me again." Then she leaned forward and started kissing the handlebars repeatedly, which made everyone in Ash's class crack up. Khalil must have been laughing too, because the camera started shaking.

Ash was too stunned to laugh. How did Lucy's bike get returned to the park? Did the thief see *The Underground News* and feel guilty about stealing it? Did a detective see their episode and quickly solve the case? Did Harry steal it himself, just so he could break the news of its return? She knew that last theory didn't make much sense, since Harry only heard about Lucy's bike after it had disappeared, but it felt good to blame Harry for stealing more than just her news report. It was easier than admitting that he'd managed—with pure luck—to turn Ash's lead into breaking news of his own.

"Tell us, Lucy," Harry said stiffly, clearly reading from pre-written notes, "do you have any tips for our viewers, based on your experience?"

"Always lock up your bike," Lucy said, "even at the playground. Thieves are *real* and they are *sneaky*. I think it's also good to tell lots of people, so they can be on the lookout. Maybe my thief returned the Yellow Flash because they heard me talking about it on a show called—"

"Thank you," Harry said, cutting her off. "Those are good tips."

Lucy smiled and resumed kissing her bike.

Ash felt her whole body tense up. She could sense Maya looking at her, but she kept staring straight ahead, forcing herself to take deep breaths.

"Thanks for coming on the show, Lucy," Damion said. "I'm Damion Skinner."

"And I'm Harry E. Levin. We hope you enjoyed this special report from *The News at Nine*, brought to you by Baltimore-based Van Ness Media." He looked right into the camera, and it felt like he was looking through it, aiming directly for Ash, as he smirked and signed off with "Have a great day."

CHAPTER 9

Showdown at Sharpener

When Harry and Damion arrived in Mr. Brooks's room and the class applauded, Ash did not join in. And when Harry went to use the pencil sharpener before math, Ash went there too, even though her pencil was mechanical.

"You're no better than that bike thief," Ash said coldly, "stealing ideas."

Harry didn't even look at her. "I don't know what you're talking about."

"You mean you weren't spying on me in the hallway?" Ash asked. "And you didn't subscribe to *The Underground News*, thebestharry11?"

Harry smiled sweetly. "Aww, thanks for saying I'm the best."

Ash could have kicked herself. She'd set herself up for that one.

"Van Ness Media thinks I'm the best too," he added. "They're going to feature me on their website."

Ash froze. Maybe she hadn't heard properly over the noise of the pencil sharpener. "What?"

"Ms. Sullivan told me today, after the show. Van Ness Media is doing a story called 'Young Creatives to Watch,' and I'm their number one news anchor. Cool, right?"

Harry held up his pencil and examined the point, which was sharp enough to stab someone in the heart. Then he smiled and went back to his seat, leaving Ash staring after him, her dull mechanical pencil loose in her hand.

CHAPTER 10

Software Company Highlights
Young Creatives to Watch

"I can't believe he was telling the truth," Ash moaned.

It was Sunday, and the Renegade Reporters had gathered at Brielle's house. They were supposed to be planning their next episode, but the feature Harry had bragged about was now live online, and it was hard to focus on *The Underground News* when *The News at Nine* anchor's smug face was filling the screen of Brielle's laptop.

"He wasn't telling the *whole* truth," Maya pointed out from the beanbag chair. "It's not like the whole story's about news anchors and Harry's number one. It's about all the different ways kids use Van Ness Media software. He's the only news anchor on there."

"Which sort of means they think he's the best," Brielle pointed out.

Ash scoffed, and Maya shot Brielle a don't-make-this-worse look, but Brielle shrugged one shoulder and said, "Just saying."

She was right. The Van Ness Media home page had a giant banner that read YOUNG CREATIVES TO WATCH accompanied by a video created using Van Ness Media software. Clicking on the banner brought up a page with detailed profiles of ten "young creatives" from around the country. A four-year-old girl who recorded original songs in Van Ness Music Studio. A fourteen-year-old boy who made his own comic books in Van Ness Art Studio. And, of course, there was "rising star" Harry E. Levin, who reported "far more than morning announcements" every school day at nine a.m.

In case the glowing description and the giant photo didn't taunt Ash enough, Harry's profile included a short clip from *The News at Nine*—from his report on Lucy and her bike.

"It's just not fair," Ash fumed. She was pacing back and forth, letting off so much steam, she could have been leaving actual smoke in her wake. "We make *The Underground News* using Van Ness Movie Maker, and they didn't want to profile me."

"Um," Brielle said, "to be precise, *I* make *The Underground News*—and *The News at Nine*—using Van Ness Movie Maker. And they didn't profile *me* either."

Ash and Maya looked at her.

"I mean, we're talking about fairness," she continued calmly, "and they're talking about software. The anchor barely touches the computer at all. Just saying."

"You're right!" said Maya with a sad look. "They should have *you* on there, Brielle, not Harry *or* Ash."

"No thanks," Brielle said quickly, holding up her hands. "I stay inside the booth for a reason. But the people on the screen always get all the credit. So it's not like any of this is fair, Ash."

Ash frowned. Brielle was right; neither show would be possible without her and her technical expertise, but the viewers barely knew she existed, let alone how hard she worked. Ash hadn't even thought about her, which only further proved Brielle's point and made Ash feel worse.

"We couldn't do anything without you, Brielle," the anchor assured her, wrapping her in a hug.

"You're the best director and editor in the world," the camerawoman added, getting up from the beanbag chair and joining in.

"Okay, okay. You two can be so extra." Brielle pushed them off and rolled her eyes. But she was smiling too. "I was just trying to say that we shouldn't take this personally. Van Ness Media probably picked Harry because it was easy, since they sponsor *The News at Nine*."

"Wouldn't they have to 'disclose' that?" Ash muttered, grumpy again at the mention of Harry. "Last year, Ms. Sullivan made me disclose that Sadie was my sister when I reported on the first-grade science projects. So people would know if I was playing favorites."

"*The Underground News* should report on favoritism at Van Ness Media," Maya joked.

But Ash didn't find it funny. In fact, Maya might be onto something. "Why *did* Van Ness Media choose Harry?" she wondered aloud. "There must be tons of kids using Van Ness Movie Maker to report the news."

"Let's see," said Brielle. She turned to her laptop and did a search for *news shows made with van ness movie maker*. Ash was happy to see Harry's face replaced by the list of results, though she noticed that there was an ad for Van Ness Movie Maker on the top, along with an ad for a bike shop.

"That's funny," Maya said, pointing to the bike ad. "Since we reported on Lucy's bike."

"Oh yeah," Brielle said as she scrolled down the page, "I've been seeing those ads everywhere ever since I edited that episode. Okay, look. Lots of news shows. This one seems like it's in Baltimore too." She clicked a link for a show called *Eager Street*, and they watched a few minutes. It was an in-depth report on pollution in the Chesapeake Bay, with a teenage anchor who was much more engaging and professional than Harry E. Levin or even, Ash had to admit, herself.

"Why would they pick Harry over this guy?" Ash said, stupefied. "How'd they choose any of the kids in the story?"

"Maybe kids submitted their projects," Maya guessed, "or their teachers did."

"Or maybe they only picked kids from schools where Van Ness Media sponsors something," Brielle tried, "like they do at John Dos Passos."

"If that's true," Ash said, "they should tell people that's the reason. Otherwise it's totally unfair. Ms. Sullivan would call it, um . . ."

"A conflict of interest," Brielle finished.

"Yes!" Ash said. "A conflict of interest. Van Ness Media only picked these people because they sponsor things at their schools. It's favoritism."

"*Maybe*," Maya reminded her. "We don't know for sure."

"Well, maybe," Ash said, "we should call them and find out."

CHAPTER 11

FEATURE:
Van Ness Media

Van Ness Media was closed over the weekend, so Ash called on Monday, right after she and Maya arrived at her house. But the phone number she found online brought her to a prerecorded menu of options, and none of them seemed quite right for her question. She hung up, frustrated.

"Who are you trying to call?" Olive asked. She was sitting on the living room floor, holding a growing number of wooden blocks, as Beckett was toddling around picking up blocks and handing them to her.

"Van Ness Media," Ash told her.

"What's that?" Olive asked.

Maya and Ash stared at her.

"You haven't heard of Van Ness Media?" Ash said incredulously. "They make apps we use at school for, like, everything."

"Really?" said Olive. "Hey, Baby Beck. Can you bring me my phone?"

Beckett looked at the blocks in his hand. Olive smiled at him and pointed to her phone, which was on the couch. Beckett carefully put the blocks down. Then he walked purposefully over to the couch, got Olive's phone, and walked it to her. She thanked him and opened her browser. "Van . . . Ness . . . Media . . ." she said, typing. "Ugh, another ad for beauty products I can't afford. You order expensive soap *one* time, and the internet thinks you're rich."

"Itch," Beckett repeated.

"Rich!" Olive said dramatically. "Okay. I'm on the Van Ness Media webpage. Here we go. 'Van Ness Media is the fastest growing creator of educational media software in the United States,'" she read. "'Our innovative, user-friendly programs teach real-life digital media skills and allow children as young as three to create professional-quality television shows, movies, music, fine art, presentations, slideshows, newsletters, and more.'"

"You sound like you're in an ad," Maya said with a giggle.

"I wish," Olive said. "Are they casting?" She flashed a smile and read the slogan from their website. "*Van Ness Media. Powered by kids' imaginations.*"

"You really hadn't heard of them before?" Ash asked. "Didn't you use Van Ness Media when you were in school?"

"Nope," Olive said to Ash, followed by "Thank you," to Beckett, who'd resumed handing her more blocks. "I'm what—twelve years older than you and Maya? We didn't have Van Ness anything when I was a kid."

"What programs did you have on your tablets?" Maya asked.

"Maybe they had actual tablets," Ash joked, "with chalk. And for writing on paper every desk had one of those dipping things . . . inkwells."

"Inkwells?" Olive said in an old-lady voice. "I wish! We wrote on cave walls with pterodactyl blood!" Then, back to herself, she did some more searching on her phone. "Check it out. Van Ness Media has only been around ten years."

She handed her phone to Ash, who took over reading aloud. "'Van Ness Media was founded in 2009 by Maria Van Ness, a Baltimore native and graduate of the University of Maryland. After teaching middle school media classes for many years, she was unsatisfied with the software available to her students and set out to create her own products. What started as one video-editing program in one classroom has since grown into a full suite of educational software used in more than three hundred thousand classrooms nationwide.'"

"Wow," Olive said. "That's a lot of classrooms."

"They're still based in Baltimore, though," Ash said. Harry E. Levin reminded her of that every single morning. "Their 'world headquarters' is in Harbor East. And listen to this! 'Maria Van Ness lives in Federal Hill with her St. Bernard, named Bernard.'"

"Holy moly," Maya said. "She lives in our neighborhood?"

"Ohhh," Olive said, tapping two blocks together. "I read

about that. She moved to Fed Hill recently, like a few weeks ago. I definitely remember reading something about a big-shot businesswoman buying a fancy row house near here."

"I don't think I've ever seen her, though," Ash said. "Have you?" She turned the phone around to show Olive and Maya a photo of a middle-aged woman with silver hair swooped across her forehead. She was wearing a pair of black pants, a black shirt, and a puffy black vest. The picture was taken at Federal Hill Park, which was right near Brielle's house. Maria Van Ness was standing at the top of the hill by the big American flag. The downtown Baltimore skyline was behind her, and an enormous dog was by her side.

"That must be Bernard," Maya said.

"Such an original name," Olive said as she swooped up Beckett, who wanted to look at the photo too. "See the dog, Beckett?"

"Doggy," he said, pointing. "Woof woof."

"That's right," Olive said. "What does a . . . cow say?"

But Beckett was too busy pointing to the dog. "Woof woof," he said again.

Ash still wanted to talk to someone at Van Ness Media to get to the bottom of their Young Creatives to Watch list. Why take her chances pressing various buttons on the phone when the founder and CEO was just across the harbor?

"Let's go to the Van Ness Media headquarters now," the anchor suggested. "We can say we're doing a story for *The*

Underground News. Maybe I can get an interview with Maria Van Ness herself!"

"You want to just go over there," Olive said, "and ask to meet the head of the company?"

"Ash is brave like that," Maya said proudly. "I don't even like when my mom makes me order my own food at a restaurant."

Ash knew that was true; she'd eaten out with Maya's family. Her mom always made her tell the waiter what she wanted herself, even though it made Maya so nervous that she'd once blurted out "calamari" instead of "macaroni." She was too embarrassed to correct herself or send it back. On the plus side, it turned out that fried squid tastes better than it sounds.

"They're right there in Harbor East," Ash said. "We can take the free water taxi. Beckett would *love* that. Wouldn't you, Baby Beck? Boat ride?"

Beckett instantly forgot about the dog. Riding the water taxi was one of his favorite things to do. "Boat!" he said, clapping his hands.

Olive looked at her watch. "Well . . . Sadie's having dinner at Lucy's, and the water taxi runs until seven. . . ."

"Yes," Ash hissed. She looked at Maya, eyebrows raised.

"I should probably check with my mom," the camerawoman said. She fired off a text message, and got a reply less than a minute later. "She said it's okay. She can even pick us all up on her way home from work."

Olive shrugged. "All right. Let's do it."

Ash zipped up her boots, ready for action. Harry E. Levin's show was "brought to you by Van Ness Media"? It was time for Ash to bring Van Ness Media to hers.

CHAPTER 12

Visit to Headquarters
Leaves Reporters Stunned, Shocked

The Underground News team didn't exactly look like a group of professional broadcast journalists as they disembarked the water taxi in Harbor East. Olive got off first, a giant diaper bag swinging from her shoulder. She unfolded the stroller and strapped in a squirming Beckett, which made his happy mood flip to anger. He kicked, reached toward the water taxi, and cried. The people waiting to board the boat made no secret of their impatience, but Ash still waited for Maya to get the camera on and ready before getting off the boat herself. It would make good background footage, as long as Brielle could edit out the sound of Beckett's crying. Then Olive pulled up the exact location of Van Ness Media on her phone and pointed in the right direction. The four of them finally set off: anchorwoman, camerawoman, screaming baby, and babysitter.

Harbor East was much newer than Federal Hill. Instead of narrow brick row houses and small, cozy shops, there were glass skyscrapers, mall-size stores, and large restaurants.

The sidewalks were full of people dressed in crisp business attire, and most of them walked briskly around *The Underground News* parade without even looking up from their phones. Ash knew it was just a coincidence that some big clouds had rolled in right when they'd gotten off the water taxi, but the drop in sunlight and temperature suddenly lent an ominous air to this outing. The anchorwoman shivered. She stuffed her hands in the pockets of her school uniform khakis and stiffened her shoulders, but she kept walking.

After a brief stop by a large fountain, which, thankfully, made Beckett forget to be upset about leaving the boat, they walked two more blocks and found themselves outside a tall, modern building with the words *Van Ness Media* wrapped around the side. While Maya shot the building from different angles, Ash stared at the entrance and wondered what on earth she was going to say once she went inside. Was she really going to accuse the CEO of playing favorites? Was it too late to turn around?

"You're going to be great," Maya whispered, gently squeezing Ash's arm.

As if on cue, a man in a suit opened the door from inside. He was about to walk through it, but he waited when he saw Ash and Maya, and said, "Coming in?"

Ash had no choice but to nod, thank him, and step inside.

"Whoa," she whispered.

The lobby was cold and cavernous. The floors were made of polished concrete. Rough, blocky columns rose to the towering ceiling. To the right, two sleek leather sofas faced each other on a large, cow-skin rug. No one was sitting on the sofas, which wasn't surprising; they didn't look very comfortable. On the other side was a row of security turnstiles, like the ones Ash had gone through that time she rode the metro in Washington, DC. A group of men passed through on their way out, each pressing an electronic badge to a sensor in order to open the glass gate. Maya was scanning the large space, and Ash could tell that she was itching to capture it on camera, but after the dancing gym teacher incident, she wouldn't dare record anything without explicit permission.

Ash's eyes were drawn to a large TV screen on the wall that was tuned to CNN. That anchor was interviewing a woman with swooping silver hair. Underneath her were the words *MARIA VAN NESS, FOUNDER AND CEO, VAN NESS MEDIA.*

"Tell me," said the CNN anchor, "why are so many schools choosing to buy your software when there are other programs with similar functionality, often available for free?"

"Great question," Maria Van Ness replied. "First of all, I believe our software is the best digital media software out there, probably for any market, but without a doubt for the education market. It's functional, it's user-friendly, and it's well-designed. But we *are* targeting the education market—kids ages three through eighteen—which means we have an extra responsibility to protect our users. Sure, there's free software available. But it's not really free. It's being paid for by advertising, which means users are being constantly bombarded by ads, whether they realize it or not. And not realizing it is when it's most harmful, especially to children. Van Ness Media products are proudly free of advertising. We aim to make money by selling software, not our customers' attention spans. That's important to schools, and rightfully so. Our commitment to having zero advertising within our products sets us apart, and it's helped us grow."

Ash liked Maria Van Ness. She was poised and eloquent and clearly very smart. She seemed to really care about kids, especially when she talked about that advertising stuff. Ash imagined herself sitting across from Maria Van Ness on CNN. She'd ask about a conflict of interest when it came to Harry, and Maria Van Ness would acknowledge her wrongdoing. *I am sincerely sorry for not disclosing my connection to his show*, the CEO would say graciously. *Thank you, Ashley, for bringing this issue to the attention of the world.*

Maya tapped Ash's shoulder, pulling her out of her daydream and back into the cold lobby. The camerawoman motioned to the far end of the room, where there was a long counter with three women behind it, two in business clothes and one in a security uniform. If Ash had any chance of turning that daydream into a reality, it would start with approaching that desk.

"Go ahead," Olive said. "Beckett and I will wait here."

They'll be happy to talk to you, Ash told herself. *Their company is "powered by kids' imaginations."* She nodded at Maya, who faithfully followed her across the room.

"Can I help you?" one of the women asked.

"Um, yes. I'm Ashley Simon-Hockheimer from *The Underground News.* This is my friend Maya. She operates the camera."

The receptionist raised one eyebrow over the wire frames of her large glasses. She seemed to be suppressing an amused smile, like Ash had just said her favorite food was "pasghetti." Like having a TV show was *cute.* It wasn't the right first impression from a company that taught kids how to make TV shows.

Ash stood up straighter and spoke more assertively. "We'd like to speak to someone about your feature on young creatives to watch. Would it be possible to interview Maria Van Ness?"

"You'd like to interview Maria Van Ness," the woman said, no longer bothering to hide her amusement, "for . . . what did you say? A book report?"

Ash and Maya exchanged glances. Who said anything about a book report?

"No," Ash said, trying to remain patient. "For our TV show. *The Underground News.* About your story about young creatives to watch. One of the people featured was from a show sponsored by Van Ness Media, and we think there might be a conflict of interest."

"A conflict of interest," the woman repeated, clearly trying to stifle a laugh.

Now Ash was getting really annoyed. This receptionist was treating her like a baby. It didn't help that the lobby was suddenly filled with the cries of an actual baby; Beckett was trying to escape from his stroller.

The other receptionist, a redhead with straight-cut bangs, stood up. "Sorry. The CEO isn't in the office today."

"CEO stands for chief executive officer," the rude receptionist explained with a patronizing smile.

"I'm sorry," the redhead said again. "She's actually in New York this week, doing a number of TV interviews." The friendly receptionist motioned to the large TV screen, where Maria Van Ness was still on (live, apparently). "You can try emailing," she continued, handing over a business card. "Or if you want to leave your own card or a note, I'll make sure it gets to the right person."

"Um," Ash said. She fumbled in the pockets of her khakis, as though they might magically contain her own business card. But of course they didn't, and Ash wasn't sure what to do. To make matters worse, Beckett's screams were now echoing off the concrete walls. Olive had taken him out of the stroller and was bouncing him up and down, but he was inconsolable.

"Why don't you just write your contact info on here," the redhead said, sliding a piece of paper and a pen across the sleek counter.

Before Ash could write anything, Olive came up behind her with a howling Beckett in her arms.

"I'm so sorry to interrupt," Olive said, "but this boy desperately needs a diaper change. Is there a restroom I can use?"

"To the left," answered the rude receptionist, wrinkling her nose.

"There's no changing table in that restroom, though," the security guard piped up. "There's not one on this floor at all."

The rude receptionist sighed. But the nice one walked over to the row of security turnstiles. "Here." She held a badge to one of the sensors, and the glass panels opened. "Go up to the fourteenth floor and make a right. There's a really nice bathroom there, with a changing table."

"Thank you so much," Olive sang, hurrying through the gate. "Let's go, Baby Beck."

But Beckett turned in her arms and reached for Ash. "Ashee!" he cried.

The nice receptionist opened the gate again. "Go ahead." She motioned Ash and Maya through. "Fourteenth floor."

They all thanked her as they hurried through the gates and into the elevator, away from the rude receptionist's look of disgust. Ash took Beckett from Olive and held his hand to the panel of buttons in the elevator. "Fourteen," she said, pointing Beckett's finger to the number. But he was too worked up to want to press it. Ash couldn't blame him.

Now that she was holding him herself—in an enclosed space, no less—it was *very* clear that his diaper was full. When the doors opened, Ash handed him back to Olive, who ran to the right, leaving the reporters to gape at the fourteenth floor.

"Holy moly," Maya whispered. "*This* is the place that sponsors *The News at Nine*?"

Ash couldn't believe it either. It seemed like someplace you'd have to pay to go to, not someplace that would pay you.

It was an enormous space with high ceilings, exposed brick, and shiny floors. In the center of the room, there was a U-shaped coffee bar with people making and sipping fancy drinks. To the left were different types of chairs and couches, all artfully arranged around tables of various shapes and sizes. To the right of the café were more tables, only these were for playing: Ping-Pong, billiards, and shuffleboard. Beyond that was a glass-enclosed studio where a handful of people were doing yoga. On a big screen above the coffee shop, Maria Van Ness was telling the CNN anchor that her employees' happiness was crucial to her company's success.

"Let's work here when we grow up," Maya whispered.

"Work here?" Ash said. "Let's *live* here. And not just when we grow up. I'm ready to move in now."

Maya giggled. "Imagine we just come back tomorrow with our sleeping bags?"

"Pulling suitcases."

"Carrying artwork to hang in our new rooms."

"And buckets of paint for our walls," Ash said with a laugh.

"With paintbrushes and rollers!" Maya said, covering her mouth.

"Imagine the look on the receptionist's face!" Ash said.

That was the final straw. They both burst out laughing so loudly, everyone turned to see what was going on. The girls looked frantically for a place they could duck out of view, but just like at Ash's house, the space was so open, there was nowhere to hide.

"Follow me," Ash said through her laughs. She walked briskly back toward the elevators. But right when she got there, the elevator doors opened and out stepped two men in coveralls carrying paint buckets, rollers, and trays. The girls started laughing so hard, they could barely breathe. Feeling the glare of every Van Ness Media employee on the fourteenth floor, Ash ran away from the café area and around the first corner she saw, Maya right at her heels. Her plan was to find the bathroom, but all she saw were offices and small meeting rooms, all with glass doors. Finally, at the end of the hall, there was a dark wooden door with no sign. It was probably a closet filled with copy paper or cleaning products, but at least they could take a minute to calm down without anyone seeing them and calling security. Ash turned the metal handle and slipped inside, Maya right behind her.

They didn't find themselves in a storage closet at all. It was a meeting room, like the ones they'd seen through the glass doors. A few people were seated around an oval table. A woman in a suit was standing at the far end of the room, underneath two large screens. One of them was full of letters and numbers, and the other was showing a map with little dots flashing at various places on the streets.

"We can track location data too," the woman in the suit was saying, "if children log in at home, or on our mobile apps. It's all connected to each user's unique profile ID—" Then she stopped, because everyone had turned to look at Maya and Ash.

Ash froze, her silliness instantly switched off.

"Can I help you?" said the man closest to the door. He had a shaved head, white glasses, and a trim beard.

"I'm sorry," Ash said. "We were, um, looking for the bathroom." But her eyes kept glancing at the big screen. The map. She knew those streets.

The man with the beard followed her gaze. "Turn it off," he said sharply to no one in particular. The woman to his left started fumbling with her laptop.

Ash's eyes moved to the other screen. It was full of text, way too much for her to read right now, let alone understand. But on the top left, in large type, were the words *PROFILE ID* followed by a string of letters and numbers. That must have been what the presenter had been talking about when she and Maya had barged in. Something about tracking location data and every child having a unique—

"Off!" the bearded man ordered. "Now."

Someone pressed a button on the projector, and the screens turned blue. The bearded man looked at Ash and Maya without smiling. "Go out, make a left," he said coldly. "At the end of the hall, make a right. The bathroom will be on your right."

"Thank you," Ash said. "Sorry again."

"We're so sorry," Maya whispered.

The girls turned and slipped back through the door as quickly as they'd entered. They walked briskly back through the hall. Neither of them said anything, but Ash could tell that Maya's head was spinning, just like her own, as she tried to process what they'd seen.

"There you are!" said Olive, who was waiting by the elevators. Beckett was quiet in her arms, happily munching on a rice cake. "Are you ready to go?"

Both reporters nodded silently.

"What a cool place to work, huh?" Olive said as they rode the elevator down. "It's so big, though. I'd need a map to find my desk."

Ash and Maya glanced at each other, and Ash knew that the only map on both their minds was the one they'd seen on that screen. The map that was tracking children's locations. It was a map of Federal Hill.

CHAPTER 13

ANALYSIS: Something Fishy

That night after dinner, while her parents did dishes and her sister did homework, Ash gave Beckett his bath. She enjoyed this nightly ritual most of the time, but she especially looked forward to it on nights like this when she had a lot on her mind. Speaking her thoughts out loud helped her reason through a problem; even better was hearing her own thoughts repeated back to her. And when it comes to listening to words and repeating them back, no one's better than a baby.

"Did you like riding the boat today?" Ash asked as she lowered Beckett into the water.

He found his toy boat and held it out to her. "Boat."

"You keep it," Ash said. "It's your boat."

"Beck boat."

"Yes, Beckett's boat. Get ready for a rinse."

Ash used one hand to cover her brother's eyes and the other to pour water over his head. Beckett twisted and splashed. He never liked that part.

"Good job, Beck. Fish?" she offered.

He blinked a few times. Then he took the toy fish and tried to force it into his mouth.

"It's not a real fish, silly."

Beckett giggled and chomped on the toy fish with more gusto.

"Okay, suit yourself." Ash pumped some baby shampoo onto her hands and rubbed it gently into his wispy hair. "So, listen to this. While you were getting a new diaper, Maya and I accidentally walked into a meeting at Van Ness Media. It was a mistake, I swear. But we saw all these adults talking about profile IDs and tracking."

"Tacking," Beckett said.

"Yeah, tracking. Whatever that means. But here's the thing. They were looking at a map of Federal Hill. *Our* neighborhood. And it had these little dots on it, like the one showing where we are when we use GPS. Do you think that's weird?"

"Eared."

"Yeah. I think it's weird too. I mean, they make the software, so I guess they're allowed to know where people are using it?"

"Ow'd," Beckett said.

"Maybe they're allowed," Ash granted. Still, something didn't feel right.

"Face," Beckett said.

"You got it. Close your eyes." As she ran a soapy wash-cloth over Beckett's face, Ash thought about the panic that had come over the room when she and Maya had walked in. It was like the way Sadie quickly closed the pantry door when Dad caught her sneaking cookies.

"Why were they in a room with no sign, at the end of a long hall," Ash wondered aloud, "when there were a million empty meeting rooms with glass doors?"

"Eyes?" Beckett asked.

"Yes, close your eyes." Ash rinsed his face with clean water. "Okay. You can open now."

He did. Then he stuffed his toy fish back in his mouth.

Someone tapped on the bathroom door.

"Come in," Ash said.

Beckett clapped and said, "Da!"

"What are you two up to in here?" Dad asked. "It sounds like quite the conversation."

"Eyes close," Beckett said seriously.

"Ah, yes," Dad said. "Eyes closed. Is that what your stimulating discussion is about?"

Ash debated telling Dad about Van Ness Media. He might have a good, structural-engineery explanation for what she'd heard.

But what if he got angry? Dad was always telling her to knock before entering. He'd even knocked now, to respect her privacy with Beckett. She and Maya hadn't meant to stumble upon a top secret meeting. Then again, they hadn't meant to stumble upon Coach Kelly dancing in her underwear either, and that had cost them *The News at Nine.* If Dad and Abba found out that Ash and Maya had seen something they weren't supposed to see—*again*—they might take away *The Underground News.*

No, she couldn't take the risk. Not when her show was only getting started, and Harry was a "Young Creative to Watch." Not when what she saw today might lead her to real news worth reporting.

"Beck and I were just talking about Van Ness Media," Ash said, which was technically true. "I think there might be a good story there."

"Ah, cool," said Dad. "Well, send them an email and see if you can get an interview lined up. That'll be better than showing up unexpected."

Too late for that, Ash thought.

"If you ask the right questions, I'm sure it'll make a great episode."

"I think so," Ash agreed. She had *lots* of questions.

Beckett held out his toy fish. "Fishy," he said.

"Yes," Ash said. She thought, *Something is very, very fishy.*

CHAPTER 14

WANTED:
Dev's Guide to Dev's Guides

"It doesn't seem that weird to me," Brielle said the next day at recess. "If I invented an app, I'd want to know where people are when they use it."

"Some of the dots were moving," Maya said eerily, as though she were telling a ghost story. "Like, these Van Ness Media people could just watch you walk along South Charles Street."

Brielle shrugged and leaned against a tree. "So what? They watch me go into Midnight Cupcakes? It's no different from, like, the traffic info on GPS."

"But Van Ness Media doesn't give people directions," Ash pointed out.

Brielle shrugged again. "Maybe they're making a new program. Van Ness Navigator."

Ash hadn't considered that. Perhaps it was top secret until it was finished. That could be why the people were hiding in that room, and why they wanted to turn off the computer when Ash and Maya walked in. "If they are," she said, "it'd be a pretty big news story. And no one else knows about it." *Especially not Harry E. Levin,* Ash added to herself. "*The Underground News* could break it!"

"Um," said Brielle, "I think we need a little more information before we can report anything."

"I don't think it's a new app," Maya said quietly, sitting down on the grass. "I think they're collecting information about us. Companies do that sort of thing. You should see the data my brother has about the visitors to his website."

Maya's brother, Dev, was a freshman in college and basically a genius. He made study guides for all different classes and sold them online.

"What kind of data?" Ash asked, sitting down next to her.

Maya picked three blades of grass and started braiding them together. "He keeps track of what people buy, obviously," she replied. "But he has lots of other information too. He showed me once. He knows how many people visit each page, how they got there, what they click on. Stuff like that."

"For real?" Ash asked. "And he looks at it?"

"He *studies* it," Maya said. "He spends, like, *hours* looking at it."

"Why?" Brielle asked.

"I don't know," Maya said.

"Maybe he's making a Dev's Guide to studying website data," Ash said with a smile.

Maya giggled. "A Dev's Guide to Dev's Guides."

"And then he'll make a Dev's Guide to Dev's Guide to Dev's Guides."

"And a Dev's Guide to Dev's Guide—"

"Okay!" Brielle announced, raising her arms. "I have an idea."

"Is it about Dev's Guides?" Ash asked, grinning.

"It is, actually," Brielle said. "We need to do more research before we report anything about Van Ness Media. But we need to record a new episode of *The Underground News* soon, or people will forget about us."

"And it needs to be a good episode," Ash added. "Even better than Lucy's bike."

"Right. So, I think we should do a story about Dev's Guides. Do you think your brother would be up for it, Maya?"

"I can ask," Maya said. "He'll probably do it if we flatter him, like, say it's because he's such a good entrepreneur."

"A good what?" Brielle asked.

"Entrepreneur," Maya repeated with a sigh. "It means someone who started their own business."

Ash knew Maya was proud of her brother, but she also knew that Maya's family was especially proud of him, more than they were of Maya, which Ash found incredibly unfair.

"I've got it," Ash said, coming up with a way to interview

Dev without making him seem even more special. "We can do a whole series on Baltimore entrepreneurs. We can interview Dev, and some other business owners nearby. And then, once we have a few, we can use it as a way to interview Maria Van Ness and find out what they're doing with that map."

"Smart," said Brielle. "I like it."

"I wish there was a Dev's Guide to finding out what's happening at Van Ness Media," Maya said, a smile playing at her lips.

Ash grinned. "Or a Dev's Guide to Dev's Guide to finding out—"

Brielle covered her ears. "I need a Dev's Guide to dealing with people who won't stop talking about Dev's Guides."

"Or a Dev's Guide to Dev's Guide to—"

Brielle just shook her head. "The things I put up with as a Renegade Reporter."

CHAPTER 15

Reporters See Data, Smell Socks

Compared to the official headquarters of Van Ness Media, the official headquarters for DevsGuides.com was tiny, messy, and gym-sock smelly—probably because it was also Maya's brother's dorm room.

"Hey, Dev," Maya said when they arrived the next afternoon.

"Hey," Dev said, messing her hair. "Hey, Ash. Did you two come here yourselves?"

"Yeah, right," Maya said, pulling away and redoing her long braid.

"We took the bus with my babysitter," Ash explained. "She's with my sister and baby brother on that big grassy area."

"The beach?" Dev said. "Cool."

Ash looked around. She'd been on the Johns Hopkins campus a few times before, but she'd never been inside a dorm room. There were two of everything: two beds, two big dressers, two small dressers, and two desks. All of it was cluttered with clothes, used dishes, and half-eaten snacks.

Half the walls—the ones on Dev's roommate's side—were covered from floor to ceiling with photos and concert posters. But the walls on Dev's side were completely bare except for a small, printed-out class schedule near the desk.

"Is your roommate here?" Maya asked.

"No," Dev said. "Why don't you grab his chair. He won't be back for a while."

Ash began sliding the roommate's chair out from under his desk, but she stopped when she found dirty socks and a pair of boxers on the seat. "Maya!" she whispered.

"Holy moly!" Maya said, covering her face. "Dev!"

"What? Oh." He chuckled. "Just push that stuff off."

But Ash didn't want to touch anyone's boxers. She looked around for something to protect her hand and found she didn't really want to touch anything in the room.

"Here," Dev said. He came over and tilted the chair so that the boxers slid to the floor. Then he turned the chair so it'd face his computer. Ash still didn't want to sit there. But she'd seen reporters broadcast live from the middle of hurricanes, or war zones. Surely, she could put her khakis-covered butt on a dorm room chair.

"So," Ash said once she'd sat down, "Maya said you could show us some of the behind-the-scenes stuff about your website?"

"Yeah, sure. Did you want to see SEO stuff? Analytics?"

Ash and Maya looked at each other, then back at Dev, blankly.

"Remember that day," Maya said, "when you were showing me some of the information you had about who visited your site?"

Ash tried to think of what would be most helpful in terms of understanding what they might have seen at Van Ness Media. "We want to know what *you* know about the people who use your website."

"Got it. Sure." Dev sat down at his desk and pulled up a log-in page.

"Hang on," Maya said. "Let me find the best angle to record this."

Dev stopped typing and turned around. "What?"

"I'm going to record it," Maya explained. "For background footage for your episode."

Dev shook his head.

"But Maya said you wanted to be on our show," Ash said. "You'll be the first in our series about local business owners."

"Sure, yeah, I'll do that. I'll talk about my business and whatever. It'll be good publicity. But you can't record any of this analytics stuff."

"We might not even use it," Maya explained. "I just want to record everything so Brielle has lots of options for visuals when she goes to edit."

But Dev was insistent. "You can look at this stuff as my sister, but not as a reporter. The analytics can't be part of the show, not even in the background. My customers might think I'm sharing their personal information, or selling it, or—"

"Dev—" Maya started, but Ash said, "Deal."

Dev wanted to keep his data secret. The people at Van Ness Media wanted to keep their meeting secret. In both cases, it only made Ash more determined to know what it showed. And Dev seemed one argument away from backing out of the whole thing. "We'll keep the analytics off the record," the anchor promised.

Dev looked at his sister and waited. Finally, Maya sighed and handed the phone to Ash, who made a show of sticking it in the zippered compartment of her backpack.

"So," Ash said, back to business. "What information do you have about your customers?"

"Short answer?" Dev said. "Everything."

"Everything?" Maya repeated.

"Check it out." Dev's fingers flew on his keyboard, and the screen filled with maps, charts, and tables. "I'll start with the big-picture stuff. See this number? That's how many people visited DevsGuides.com in the past thirty days."

"Four *thousand*?" Ash said. "That seems like a lot."

"It's pretty good," Dev assured her. "And that's unique visitors. Counting repeats—the number of times the site was visited overall—it's over seven thousand. See?"

"Dev!" Maya said. "That's *really* good!"

"Especially for September," Dev told her. "You should see my stats in May, around final exam time."

"What was it when you first started?" Maya asked. "Like, in the very, very beginning?"

"Oh, I don't know. Ten, twenty visits a month? And mostly people from Baltimore. But now it's visitors from all over the country, even some from other countries." He pointed to a map on the screen. Numbers popped up as he ran the cursor over it. "This map shows where the visitors live, or where they were when they were looking at my site, at least. And if I click on a state"—he clicked on Florida, to demonstrate—"it will get more specific, showing me which town or city they're in."

"Can you zoom in really close?" Ash asked, thinking of the map she'd seen at Van Ness Media. "Like, could you look at the specific streets in Federal Hill and see people moving around?"

"I can only get it down to ZIP codes," Dev said, "but I'm sure other companies can get more specific."

Maya and Ash exchanged meaningful glances, but Dev didn't notice. He was pointing to the screen. "See, this circle means there were two hundred seventy visitors from Miami. If I click on it, I learn more about those visitors." He kept clicking as he talked, pulling up page after page of information. "I can see their age and gender." *Click.* "Their interests." *Click.* "How they got to my site—if they clicked on a link, for instance, or did a search." *Click.* "If they searched, I can see what they searched for." *Click.* "And then, once they got here, I can see which pages they went to, in which order. If they ended up buying a study guide, which one they bought."

"I told you it was a ton of data," Maya said to Ash. "He used to stare at it for hours a day."

"Yeah, man," Dev said. "How do you think I went from twenty visitors a month to four thousand?"

"By using this data?" Ash tried.

"Bingo!" Dev sat back in his chair and put his hands behind his head. "My study guides are good, sure. But a lot of it's because of this data. Check this out." He pointed at Ash, and then went back to the computer. "If we go to my sales stats page, I can see which guides sold the most in a given period of time. Let's look at last week." He did. "Okay, cellular biology. The purpose of cells, parts of cells, that sort of stuff. Makes sense, right? Because it's the beginning of the year, and biology classes are starting with cells."

"Oh," Ash said, "right." She didn't know anything about biology classes, but she wanted to see where this went.

"Now. Let's look at all the people who downloaded my cellular biology guide, and see where they live. Lots of them live in . . . New York. So, knowing that, I can look up the standard biology curriculum in New York, and see what the next unit is going to be. Or I can just look at my past sales and see which guide most people download about a month after they download the cellular biology one, especially people who live in New York. Let's say they usually buy my study guide for genetics next. In that case, I can wait a couple weeks and send an email to those people with a direct link to the genetics guide. Or I can run some targeted advertising on Google or Facebook."

"Targeted advertising?" Ash asked, trying to keep up.

"Ads that will only appear to certain people," Dev explained. "In this case, I could set an ad for my genetics study guide to appear on Google or Facebook specifically to people who are in ninth grade somewhere in New York. Maybe even people in ninth grade, in New York, who previously searched for things related to cellular biology."

"Like the ads for sunglasses all over our computer," Maya said, "because Mom and Massi were looking for new ones. That's called targeted advertising?"

"Bingo," Dev said.

Ash had a story of her own about that. "Last year," she said, "when it was close to my birthday, I used the computer after my dad, and there were ads for girls' boots on the side of every webpage I went to. He must have been looking at boots to get me for my birthday."

"You did get boots!" Maya said. "Your really cool gray ones."

"Yep." Ash lifted her feet. She was wearing them right

now. "Get this. Once I realized what my dad was doing, I did some searching of my own and found the exact ones I wanted. Then I made sure to visit the page with them a few times. So the next time Dad used the computer, these exact ones would appear in all the ads."

Maya looked shocked, but Dev nodded, clearly impressed. "I like it," he said. "Way to use targeted advertising to your advantage."

"I don't know," Maya said uneasily. "It's like people are spying on us."

"Like Harry in the hallway," Ash put in.

"Worse than that, because we don't even know who's doing it or when. The whole thing's just sort of . . . creepy."

"Oh, it's super creepy," Dev agreed. "Big companies are tracking everything we do, all the time."

Van Ness Media is a big company, Ash thought. *Are they keeping track of more than just locations?* "Everything?" she repeated.

"Yeah, man. Your computer has a unique IP address. So does your phone. It's kind of like a fingerprint, and it leaves a trail wherever you go online. That's actually what it's called when companies track this stuff—fingerprinting. They keep track of your searches and your posts and your purchases. Then every website has code built into it to collect and analyze that information. Like mine does. Plus, we all give tons of other information voluntarily, when we sign up for things or comment on things or post things. I know some stuff about my customers, but I'm just barely scratching the surface. If I wanted, I could buy more data. There are companies called data brokers that collect all our personal information and sell it to other companies."

"But," Maya asked, "why?"

"Because people want it," Dev said with a shrug. "The more they know about you, the more stuff they can try to sell you."

Ash shifted uncomfortably in her gray boots, thinking through what the shoe company knew about her. They knew where she lived (since her dad had to put in an address to have them shipped) and how big her feet were (from what size he ordered) and what color and style she liked (from the ones she'd picked). Then she remembered, suddenly but clearly, that one of the websites she'd looked at for boots had been advertising a sale on "pre-teen necessities," and Ash had clicked on a few training bras, just to see what they looked like. Did the company track that? She imagined a meeting like the one at Van Ness Media, only this time it was *her* personal browsing history on the big screen, and the woman in the suit was saying, "Ashley Simon-Hockheimer spent five minutes considering a white training bra, size small." Talk about mortifying.

"Do these companies keep track of what individual people do?" she asked, trying to sound casual. "Like, do they know that I, Ashley Simon-Hockheimer, looked up . . . something in particular? Or do they just know it was a girl about my age in Baltimore?"

"Depends. I know the name of anyone who buys one of my guides. Companies usually say the data they track is anonymous, but who knows? They probably keep really detailed profiles on everyone, with names and everything."

Ash swallowed. She'd heard that word before, *profile*. That's what had been on the screen at Van Ness Media during the secret meeting. Profile ID. The presenter had said each user had a unique profile ID. The location data must have been just one part of each person's profile. Brielle's theory—that they were creating a navigation app—was looking less and less likely. It seemed like all this profile stuff had to do with advertising.

But Van Ness Media didn't have any advertising in their programs. Maria Van Ness had said so in that interview. Ash remembered it clearly: *We aim to make money by selling software, not our users' attention spans.* If that was true, why would they be making profiles for all their users? Ash thought of Beckett's word during his bath: *Fishy.* There was a news story here for sure.

"Why do you guys want to know all this stuff, anyway?" Dev asked.

"Um," said Maya.

"Background research for a story," Ash finished.

"Not the story about Dev's Guides," Dev reminded them.

"We *know*, Dev," Maya said. "Holy moly. We already promised."

Ash's phone vibrated, and she took it out to find a message from Olive, asking how much longer they'd be. "Can we do the Dev's Guides story now?" she asked. "My babysitter's waiting for us."

"And the smell in here is starting to get to me," Maya added, wrinkling her nose.

"Yeah, what *is* that?" Dev asked. "I wasn't going to say anything, but it didn't smell until you two arrived."

"Yeah, right," Maya said. "Ash and I smell fine. It's your dirty clothes."

"You mean these?" Dev pulled a rumpled T-shirt off the floor and held it to Maya's nose. She shrieked and pushed him away.

"Or is it my roommate's socks?" Dev asked. He got up to reach for them, and this time both girls shrieked.

"Ew, I think it might really be his socks," Dev said, pulling his hand away. "Let's keep the smell off the record too, okay?"

But the news anchor smiled and shrugged. "No promises. We've got to report the facts."

THE UNDERGROUND NEWS, EPISODE 3

REPORTER: Ashley Simon-Hockheimer
VIDEOGRAPHER: Maya Joshi-Zachariah
EDITOR: Brielle Diamond
SLUG: Dev's Guides (Local business 1)

VIDEO	AUDIO
Anchor on Camera	**ANC:** Coming up, an exclusive interview with Dev Joshi-Zachariah, the founder and CEO of the hugely popular Dev's Study Guides. I'm Ashley Simon-Hockheimer with the Renegade Reporters, and you're watching *The Underground News*.
Intro and Credits	NONE
Anchor on Camera	**ANC:** Welcome to *The Underground News*. Today we're kicking off a new series about local businesses and successful entrepreneurs. Our first interview is with Dev Joshi-Zachariah of DevsGuides.com, which offers downloadable study guides for middle and high schoolers.
Images of DevsGuides.com	**ANC voiceover:** DevsGuides.com started just two years ago with the sale of one study guide. It now has study guides for more than fifty topics in every major subject of middle and high school, with more coming all the time.

Dev and Anchor Walking on Johns Hopkins Campus	**ANC voiceover:** The founder and creator of all the guides is Dev Joshi-Zachariah, a freshman at Johns Hopkins University. Disclosure: He also happens to be the brother of *The Underground News* videographer, Maya Joshi-Zachariah, which is how we managed to get this exclusive interview. DevsGuides.com is based in Baltimore. In fact, the founder and CEO runs it entirely from his Johns Hopkins dorm room.
Anchor and Dev in his Room	**ANC:** What gave you the idea to start DevsGuides.com? **DEV:** Starting in middle school, whenever I had a test coming, I'd sum up all my notes in one or two pages, to help myself study. Sometimes my friends would ask to borrow my review sheets, and they always said they were really helpful for the tests. Then, in high school, I started tutoring, and I'd share my study guides with the kids I tutored. Word started to spread, and suddenly, people were asking if they could buy the guides. I sold my first study guide to one family for ten bucks. The business just started growing from there.

Images of DevsGuides.com	**ANC voiceover:** And boy did it grow. The website now has more than four thousand unique visitors a month. Around midterm and final exams, that number can be as high as nine thousand. According to the *Baltimore Business Journal,* Dev's Guides is one of the fastest growing companies in Maryland. And *Baltimore Magazine* recently featured Dev in an article about up-and-coming entrepreneurs in Maryland.
Anchor and Dev in his Room	**ANC:** Your company has grown really quickly. How many people work for DevsGuides.com? **DEV:** Just one. Me. **ANC:** You don't have any employees? **DEV:** Sometimes I'll pay a friend to look over a new guide for spelling and stuff before I post it. But otherwise, I do everything. I make the guides, I run the website, I do the marketing and advertising, I deal with customer service questions. I do it all. **ANC:** And you do it all from this room? **DEV:** I have a roommate, so I do it all from my half of this room.

Sidney Hendelman at his Home	**ANC voiceover:** Sidney Hendelman is a high school sophomore, and he's one of DevsGuides most loyal customers. **SIDNEY HENDELMAN:** Oh, Dev's Guides are the best study guides out there. They just make everything really clear and easy to understand. I use them for homework, and then, on a test, I can just, like, picture the way it looks on the Dev's Guide, and remember the information.
Anchor and Sidney Hendelman at his Home	**ANC:** Have your grades gone up since you started using Dev's Guides? **SIDNEY:** Oh, for sure. See this B+ on my last math test? I used to get Cs most of the time. My parents were going to get me a tutor, but someone told them about Dev's Guides, and we decided to try that first. And then my friend Anaya actually had a tutor, and the tutor explained stuff to her using a Dev's Guide!
Anchor and Dev Walking on JHU Campus	**ANC voiceover:** Dev Joshi-Zachariah plans to continue to run and grow DevsGuides.com for as long as he can while still keeping up with his own studying. Once he graduates from Johns Hopkins, he might work on the business full-time. He says he has ideas for other ways to grow, like expanding into college-level guides or maybe SAT and ACT prep. But for now, it's enough to balance being an entrepreneur and being a college student himself.

Anchor and Dev in his Room	**ANC:** What's your best-selling study guide? **DEV:** It's interesting. Science is the most popular subject, with math a close second. Those are the most popular subjects, by far. But in terms of individual study guides, the single best seller, no contest, is my guide to *Romeo and Juliet*. **ANC:** For real? **DEV:** Yeah, man. I don't know why. Maybe because a lot of teens have to read it, or maybe because they have a hard time understanding it. Maybe it's just a good guide.
Image of *Romeo and Juliet* Guide	**ANC voiceover:** Or maybe middle and high schoolers just can't resist a good love story.
Anchor on Camera	**ANC:** Thanks for tuning in to our first episode in our new series on local entrepreneurs. I'm Ashley Simon-Hockheimer, and this is *The Underground News*.

CHAPTER 16

Rivals Clash Under the Stars

That Sunday night was the start of the Jewish new year, a holiday called Rosh Hashanah. In Baltimore, that meant it was time for Rosh Hashanah Under the Stars. Ash usually dreaded going to synagogue, since it required dressing up, sitting quietly, and waiting until the service was over to eat crumbly, flavorless cookies. But she loved Rosh Hashanah Under the Stars. It was outside in a huge park with a small playground and an enormous hill. Everyone wore jeans and sweatshirts and brought a picnic dinner to eat before and throughout the prayers. The stage with the rabbi was broadcast on a huge screen, like at an Orioles game. There were people directing traffic in the parking lot like at an Orioles game too; Rosh Hashanah Under the Stars was that popular.

"Everyone has to hold something," Dad said when they got out of their minivan. "I've got the blankets."

"I'll hold the sushi," said Ash, slipping the bag of take-out onto her wrist.

"I'll hold Beckett," said Abba, strapping on a baby carrier, "and the drinks."

"Hole keys," said Beckett, taking the car keys from Dad and stuffing them into his mouth.

"No, you won't," said Abba, taking them out and putting them in his pocket.

"I'll hold Bubbe's hand," said Sadie, waving at their grandmother, who'd just gotten out of a car nearby.

"We brought dessert!" said their grandfather, holding up a container of brownies.

They were all holding too much to give each other hugs, but they did lean in for kisses and say "Shana tovah," happy new year, before setting off toward the park.

Ash was always amazed by the number of people at this service. There weren't many Jewish people where she lived in Federal Hill, so the events downtown were always small, with the same four or five families. But there were a lot more Jewish people in this part of Baltimore, and Rosh Hashanah was a major holiday. Abba pulled up an article on his phone (which, Ash noticed, had an ad for sushi right in the middle) that said there would be more than six thousand people attending this service, a figure so big Ash could hardly wrap her head around it. But she especially couldn't wrap her head around why, with six thousand people in a giant park, her family ended up putting their picnic blanket next to the one with the only other Jewish sixth grader at John Dos Passos Elementary School: Harry E. Levin.

"Shana tovah," Dad said to Harry's mom, Dr. Chan.

"Happy new year," she replied.

The grown-ups started chatting. Ash busied herself with setting up dinner, hoping to avoid talking to Harry. But Harry came right over to her and started talking.

"Hey, Ash," he said. "What are you doing for your portfolio?"

"What portfolio?" she asked, arranging the sushi containers in a line.

"Our quarterly portfolio. For school."

Ash frowned at the spicy tuna roll. The quarterly portfolio wasn't due for another month, at least. She had more important things to work on before then. "I don't know," she said. "Why?"

"Just wondering," Harry said. He sat down on her blanket, making himself comfortable. *Too* comfortable, Ash thought.

"I'm going to put all my work in a slideshow with music," he continued. "I've been working on it at home, trying it with different songs. Want to see what I've got so far?"

He pulled out his phone and opened the Van Ness Presentations app.

Tracking, Ash thought. If Harry opened his portfolio right now, would that be represented by a little dot on a map at the Van Ness Media headquarters? Would it be added to his unique user profile? *Harry E. Levin spent Sunday night at Oregon Ridge Park celebrating Rosh Hashanah.* What else did Van Ness Media know about him?

"What are you putting in your slideshow?" Ash asked as she opened small containers of soy sauce.

"All the stuff Mr. Brooks said. Classwork, projects, art. But you're supposed to give it a personal touch. So I'm going to put really good music in the background, and edit it with, like, quick cuts." Harry took a pair of chopsticks, split them apart, and starting using them like drumsticks on the side of a sushi container. "I've already got some footage of me drumming and anchoring *The News at Nine*. Let me show you."

Harry was her rival. He had spied on her in the hallway and stolen her story about Lucy. But it still didn't seem right that Van Ness Media was spying on *him* without him knowing. Ash couldn't let him open the app and not say anything.

"Hang on," she said. "Do you think the people at Van Ness Media know what you're putting in your portfolio?"

"What?" Harry looked like Ash had just asked him to pay for all the sushi. "What are you talking about?"

"Like . . ." Ash fumbled for the right words. Maybe she should start at the beginning. "So, I saw the thing about young creatives to watch, and I couldn't figure out why Van Ness Media picked *you*."

She knew those were the wrong words the instant they came out of her mouth, even before Harry's face confirmed it. But it was too late to put them back in. "That's not what I—"

"Not what you meant?" Harry interrupted. "Yeah, right." He scoffed. "What *happened* to you, Ash? You used to be kind of cool, but this year you're so jealous of me, you can't even talk about anything else."

"What happened to *me?*" Ash said, incredulous. It was a good thing he'd interrupted her when he did. Had she really been about to try and help Harry E. Levin? "What happened to *you?* Ever since you became lead anchor, you've been mean and braggy and obnoxious."

"Whatever," Harry said, looking down at the blanket. "You're just jealous."

"I'm not," Ash insisted. "I *was*, fine, but I'm not anymore. I have *The Underground News* now, and we're investigating something about Van Ness Media that might be a big story."

"You're lying," Harry said.

"I'm not," Ash said again. She glanced at her dads to make sure they weren't listening. They were still talking to Harry's parents. Even so, Ash leaned closer to Harry and lowered her voice. "Maya and I went to the Van Ness Media headquarters in Harbor East, and we saw something important. It's way bigger than you and the stupid *News at Nine*, okay? So don't worry about me being *jealous*."

Harry glared at her, clearly furious that she'd called his show stupid. Ash glared back with slightly less venom, like she knew she shouldn't have used that word but was too mad to apologize.

"Shana tovah, everyone," came the rabbi's voice through the speakers. "We're going to begin our service in five minutes."

"We'd better start eating," Ash's grandmother said. "Excuse me, Ashley. I'm going to have some sushi." She took a plate and some chopsticks and began to serve herself. The rest of Ash's family followed, crowding between the rival anchors and their dueling glares.

"Come here, Harry," Dr. Chan said from the next blanket over. "Let's let them eat."

But Harry stepped between Sadie and Abba to be closer to Ash. "Van Ness Media sponsors *my* show," he said quietly but firmly. "And *I* was their number one news anchor to watch."

Ash pressed her lips together and her arms to her chest.

"So, if you're not lying, and there *is* big news about Van Ness Media," Harry said, "*you're* not going to break it. *The News at Nine* will get there first."

CHAPTER 17

Reporters Dig Deep, Break Through

Harry's threat kicked the Renegade Reporters' investigation into high gear. Maya volunteered to learn more about how companies track personal data online. Her brother was pleased with how his interview came out, so he was happy to help. Brielle offered to dig into the Van Ness Media software itself. She poked around the apps at school and at home to figure out what, exactly, users agreed to and how their personal information was stored. That left Ash to research Maria Van Ness. She spent the week reading articles, watching interviews, and learning as much as she could about the Van Ness Media founder and CEO.

On Saturday afternoon, they all met at Maya's house to share what they had learned.

Ash walked up just as Brielle was being dropped off. "I came *this* close to stepping in dog poo on my way here," Ash said with a shudder.

"Someone on my street put up a sign that says *Pick up after your pet*," Brielle said. "Then the dog pooped right in front of it."

The door to Maya's house opened just wide enough for the girls to see Maya's head. She looked left and right, then hurried her friends inside and closed the door quickly behind them.

"The dog poo bandit is still on the loose," Ash reported.

But Maya clearly had bigger concerns. "Did you bring your phones?" she asked.

"Yeah, of course," Ash said, taking hers out of her jacket pocket.

"Turn them off," Maya said.

"What?" Brielle said, making it very clear that she wouldn't.

"They're tracking devices," Maya said. "Please turn them off?"

"I probably shouldn't," Ash said. "My dads want me to leave it on for emergencies."

"Can you at least turn off the location settings, then?" Maya pleaded.

"Okay," Ash said slowly, "but I don't know how."

"Here." Brielle took Ash's phone, moved her thumb around the screen, and handed it back. "I'm leaving mine on, though," she said, "because this just seems extra."

Maya was clearly unhappy, but she didn't argue.

"Maya," Ash said, "are you okay?"

"Not really." Maya started walking upstairs. "I'm glad I don't have a smartphone. This tracking stuff is creeping me out."

"Um, yeah, we can tell," Brielle said, following her.

In all the years Ash had been friends with Maya, she'd never seen her this nervous. The feeling was contagious, like a yawn. It made Ash's legs tremble as she lowered herself onto Maya's bed. "Tell us what you found out."

"Yeah, you go first," Brielle said, sitting cross-legged on the floor. "Gum?"

Ash took a piece, but Maya shook her head. She got a notebook from a drawer of her nightstand and joined Ash on the bed. "Basically," she began, "people are spying on us all the time."

"That's what your brother showed you guys, right?" Brielle said, unimpressed. "That companies track what everyone does online, and they use it to make detailed profiles about people?"

"Yes, but there's so much more," Maya said. "The GPS in your phone knows that you went from your house to my house just now, and so do any apps that have access to your location—that's why I said to turn it off. If any apps have access to your microphone, they could be recording what we say right now, without us knowing. It doesn't even matter if you don't have a smartphone, like me. Smart speakers do it too. And there are cameras in public places and in smart doorbells recording people, and then facial recognition software can tell you who those people are."

"Let's use that footage to catch the dog poo bandit!" Ash joked, trying to lighten the mood.

But Maya kept it heavy. "Every single thing you do is being recorded, everywhere. Like, when you're inside a store, there are these things called 'Bluetooth beacons' that interact with your phone to track what you do, even if your Bluetooth is off! Like, if you spend a long time by the potato chips, you might start seeing ads for potato chips."

Brielle tapped her hands on the floor. "I was in the supermarket with my granddad yesterday, and he couldn't decide which yogurt to buy, regular or Greek. Then, when we were waiting to check out, he all of a sudden got a coupon for Greek yogurt on his phone!"

"For real?" Ash asked.

"Mm-hmm. We thought it was a crazy coincidence."

"Did you buy Greek yogurt?" Maya asked nervously.

"Yeah! We had regular in the cart, but I ran back to switch it so we could use the coupon."

This was too much for Maya. Her body deflated like a balloon until she was lying flat on her back, her hands over her face.

"It could have just been a crazy coincidence," Ash tried, chewing her gum slowly.

Maya shook her head behind her hands. "It wasn't."

"Well," Brielle said, "it is a *little* creepy, but it's also good. I mean, my dad wouldn't be able to get anywhere without GPS. And my granddad saved a dollar on that yogurt."

Maya peeked through her fingers. "A dollar? You'll let companies track your every move for one dollar?"

"They're not tracking my *every* move," Brielle said, rolling her eyes. "Well, I actually don't really know, because I tried to read the privacy policy for Van Ness Movie Maker, and it was impossible to understand. It was like one of those reading comprehension tests, only ten times longer, and a million times harder." Brielle took out her phone—which made Maya wince—and pulled up a file she'd saved. "Like, listen to this. It's on page thirteen, which isn't even the last page." She placed her gum on her pinky and then began to read. " 'In respect of processing of Personal Data detailed in this Privacy Policy, such processing is necessary for the purposes of a legitimate interest pursued by Van Ness Media, and we have assessed that such interests are not overridden by the interests or fundamental rights and freedoms of the persons to whom the Personal Data relates.' I mean, huh?"

The looks on Ash's and Maya's faces expressed the same reaction. Ash had no idea what that meant. She asked for Brielle's phone and reread that paragraph to herself a couple times. "Legitimate interest pursued by Van Ness Media," she mumbled.

"*Legitimate* was one of our spelling words last year," Maya remembered. "It means valid, reasonable, or fair."

Ash read the sentence to herself again. "So, I think this means that Van Ness Media can use our personal data for whatever they decide is a good reason."

"Whatever *they* decide is a good reason," Maya repeated. "*We* get no say."

"Well, we sort of do," Brielle pointed out, putting her gum back in her mouth. "We have to click the box to accept the terms and conditions when we sign up for the program or app."

"Oh," Ash said. "Is *that* what that's for?" Whenever she wanted to use something new on her computer or phone, a screen would pop up with a long document in small type. She always just scrolled to the bottom of it and hit the accept button without reading any of it. Sometimes there was no document, just a link to one, and Ash always hit accept without bothering to click the link. "What happens if you don't click the box to accept?" she asked Brielle.

Brielle shrugged. "Then you can't use the app."

"See? That's unfair," Maya said. "It's all or nothing. Either you let them collect your personal information and do whatever they want with it, or you can't use the app at all."

"Good point," Ash agreed. "They get to make the rules. If there were a button that let you use the app without giving up your personal information, I bet a lot of people would click it. What do the companies use our information for, anyway?"

"Ads, mostly," Maya said hopelessly.

"Honestly?" Brielle said slowly. "I don't see why that's so bad."

Maya stared at her like she'd said she didn't see why drowning kittens was so bad.

But Brielle just leaned back and popped her gum. "Ads are everywhere anyway, right? They always have been. All this data stuff just helps the ads get to people who might want to see them. It's pretty cool tech, actually. I'd rather see ads for things I might want to buy than ads for things I don't care about. And yeah, maybe they know some stuff about me, but so what? It's not like I have something to hide."

"Sometimes you do," Ash pointed out. "What if Harry was secretly recording our conversation right now? He could use it to steal our story again."

"We're not talking about *Harry*," Brielle argued. "We're talking about computers at big companies that record our info, turn it into ones and zeroes, and spit out ads. Who cares?"

Maya, speechless, looked at Ash to back her up. So did Brielle. But Ash was caught in the middle. On the one hand, Brielle had a point. Ads were all around, and more relevant ads could work in everyone's favor, like they did when Ash wanted gray boots, or when Dev wanted to let high schoolers know about a new study guide.

On the other hand, Abba had recently made Ash pick out a stick of deodorant for herself, which was embarrassing enough while it was happening. What if Van Ness Media had noticed that her specific location dot had spent time in the deodorant aisle of CVS and sent her a coupon for another stick? What if it said "We know your armpits are smelly!" and it popped up while she was using a Van Ness program at school, where other kids could see it?

Thankfully, she remembered that that specific nightmare could never happen—because of a fact that should reassure Maya too. "Van Ness Media doesn't allow any advertising in their programs! There isn't a single ad in any app. Maria Van Ness mentions that in basically every interview she does. It's one of their biggest selling points to schools." Ash took out her phone and tried to pull up the links to interviews she'd read. But she'd saved the links in Van Ness Writer, and the app wouldn't load.

"Huh," Ash said, showing her friends the screen. "It won't let me open Van Ness Writer unless I turn my location settings back on."

Maya gasped. "See? They want to track your location."

"So what?" Brielle said, getting annoyed. "They don't allow ads."

"Okay," Ash said loudly, the key question becoming clear. "They don't allow ads, but they're still recording our location—and probably everything else we do—to keep profiles on us. *Why?*"

They all sat there in silence for a good thirty seconds. Then Brielle took out her phone and began to scroll through the Movie Maker privacy policy. Maya paged through printouts of articles Dev had sent her. Ash pulled up the photo of Maria Van Ness with her dog in Federal Hill Park. Ironically, it was soon blocked by a popup ad for Van Ness Media. *VAN NESS MEDIA: POWERED BY KIDS' IMAGINATIONS.*

Something popped for Ash and it wasn't her gum. *Powered by kids' imaginations.* What if that wasn't just a slogan? What if kids' imaginations—and their notes, and their creations, and their physical locations—were powering Van Ness Media's rapid-fire growth?

"Remember when we were interviewing Dev," Ash said slowly, "and he didn't want us to get any of his analytics on camera? He said he didn't want his customers to think he was sharing their personal information—or *selling* it."

"Oh yeah," said Maya. "There are companies that buy data from websites and sell it to advertisers and stuff. They're called"—she looked through her notes until she found it—"data brokers. Data brokers buy and sell our personal information without us knowing."

"And it's worth a lot of money?" Brielle asked.

"Tons."

"Enough to pay for a fancy headquarters in Harbor East with coffee and Ping-Pong and yoga rooms?" Ash said.

Maya's eyes widened. Brielle cocked her head, like they'd finally hit on something interesting.

"Van Ness Media doesn't let any advertising come *in*," Ash said, piecing her thoughts together.

Maya picked up those pieces and completed the connection. "But they could still let their users' personal information go *out*."

"So that means . . ." said Ash.

"Van Ness Media . . ." said Brielle.

"Is selling our personal details to the highest bidder!" announced Maya.

That's it! They'd got it. And they could report it long before Harry. Ash felt triumphant. Until she replayed the news in her mind, letting it sink in.

Then she felt sick.

CHAPTER 18

Investigators Create Fake Person, Account

It was Maya who came up with the theory. It was Brielle who pointed out that even if it was right, they didn't have any hard proof. It was Ash who thought of a way to get that proof: Create a new Van Ness Media account and fill it with specific information. If Van Ness Media was selling that information to other companies, the computer they used to create the account would soon be filled with ads for things their fake person had mentioned.

So, the very next day, the Renegade Reporters gathered again, this time at Brielle's house, to create a fake account. The frightened Maya from the day before seemed to have been swapped overnight with a confident, determined Maya. She brought Dev's old laptop, which he agreed to let them use for the investigation. "He reformatted it before he left for college," Maya said, "so it doesn't have any of his personal information on it. But he said that before we create the account, we should still"—she checked a page of handwritten notes—"use a new browser, and clear the cookies."

"Clear the cookies!" Ash said. "Where are they? I'll eat them."

"Not real cookies," Brielle explained as she set up the browser according to those instructions. "Digital cookies. They're little text files that websites put on your computer. But now I want real cookies too. We have some Berger cookies downstairs."

Ash's stomach rumbled at the thought of Berger cookies, specifically the thick layer of fudgy icing that topped them.

"Focus," Maya said, placing a steady hand on the anchor's shoulder. "We can have Berger cookies at lunch. After we prove our theory."

"My mom said she'd order pizza too," Brielle said.

Pizza and Berger cookies? Ash could barely wait.

"The lighting and sound are good," Maya said.

"And the browser's ready," Brielle said, stepping away from the laptop.

"Cool." Ash rubbed her hands together. "Let's do this."

The editor positioned herself behind the camera and assumed her directorial voice. "Footage for the fake account in three . . . two . . ."

The anchor looked at the camera. "We're creating our fake Van Ness Media account on this laptop. It was completely reformatted, so there's no personal information on it. In order to make sure ads aren't targeted using old searches, we're using a new browser that we just installed on this computer. As an extra precaution, we cleared the cookies."

Proud of herself for keeping a straight face about cookies, Ash turned to the laptop. She opened the browser, went to the Van Ness Media software page, and clicked on LOG IN TO BEGIN CREATING. "Here's the welcome screen," the anchor said, pointing. "New users click here." The next screen listed all the programs you could access with your Van Ness Media account, along with prices for individuals and links to information for schools. "It's a good thing they offer new users a one-week free trial. We don't have much of a budget here at *The Underground News*."

The editor rolled her eyes. The videographer tried not to giggle. The anchor continued on.

"Now it's time to put in some personal information for our fake user."

Ash clicked in the box for first name and paused. They'd decided to create a fake user, but that was as far as they'd gotten. "Our user will be . . . a boy . . . named . . ." Ash glanced at her crew, but they looked just as blank as her mind was. So she went with the name of the street they were on. "Warren," she said, typing it in. "Warren . . . G. Harding."

"Cut!" said Brielle. "Warren G. Harding is the name of a president."

"No wonder it sounded so good!" Ash said. "I thought it had a real ring to it."

Maya giggled. "We need to think of a different name."

"How about Andrew . . ." Ash said, "Jackson."

Brielle snorted. "He was a president too!"

"I've got it," Ash said. She turned to the laptop and typed in *George Washington*.

"Stop!" Maya said. She was full-on laughing now. "Stop naming presidents."

"Their names just sound so real," Ash explained. "All the other names I can think of sound made up. Like . . . Maximillian Goldenfarber."

Brielle looked at her over her glasses. "You jumped from George Washington to Maximillian Goldenfarber?"

Ash tried again. "Bink Winkleman?"

Maya sank to the floor in a heap of laughter.

Brielle cried, "Think of something common and boring!"

"John . . ." Ash started.

"There you go."

"Smith," Ash finished.

Brielle shook her head. "That's so real it sounds fake."

Maya laughed so hard, she started crying.

"You try!" Ash said to Brielle.

Brielle looked her straight in the eye. Without hesitating or even blinking, she said, "Michael Conway."

Maya could barely catch her breath. "He goes to our school!" she panted.

"He does?" Brielle asked.

Ash did her best impression of the main office lady. "Michael Conway, report to the main office. Michael Conway to the main office."

"You're right!" Now Brielle was laughing too. "I knew it sounded familiar. How about Joseph . . . Taylor."

"He goes to our school too!" Maya cried before rushing out of the room and into the bathroom, which made Ash and Brielle break down in hysterics.

When Maya came back and they all calmed down, the team finally came up with a name that sounded real and didn't belong to anyone they knew from school or history: Jacob Brown. Realizing they needed more information to create Jacob Brown's Van Ness Media account, they got him an email address and decided on his birthday. They checked the box to accept the terms and conditions (which had a link to the same incomprehensible privacy policy they'd already seen), and then clicked submit.

A new screen popped up.

"'We see that you're twelve years old,'" Ash read aloud for the camera. "'That's great! Van Ness Media products are made especially for kids. But we do need to make sure an adult says it's okay for you to sign up. Please provide your parent or guardian's email address here.'"

The team looked at one another. They hadn't expected this step.

"Cut," Brielle said.

Maya did, then said, "Uh-oh. What do we do now?"

"We create an email account for Jacob Brown's parent or guardian," Brielle answered, "then open the email and say it's okay for Jacob Brown to sign up."

Ash shifted nervously. She already felt kind of slimy for pretending to be a person who didn't exist. Pretending to be that person's parent or guardian felt like an even worse form of lying. One glance at Maya confirmed that she was uncomfortable with it too; she looked like she might need to run to the bathroom again, this time because she was sick.

"I guess it's not that different from 'Jacob Brown' agreeing to the terms and conditions himself?" Ash said uneasily.

"Exactly," said Brielle. "It's not like Jacob Brown's parents would spend a couple hours reading the terms and conditions."

"Or be able to change them," Maya pointed out with a sigh.

Even so, Ash's palms were suddenly clammy.

Maya took a breath and stood up straighter, summoning her courage. "We've got to do it, so we can find out for sure what's going on. If we don't, our investigation ends here."

Ash didn't want that to happen. She knew their theory about Van Ness Media was right, and she knew it would be a huge story for *The Underground News*. But they couldn't report it if they couldn't prove it, and Harry E. Levin was probably researching Van Ness Media right now, determined to find and break the story himself. Would her rival anchor think twice about creating an email address for a fake person's fake parents? Not a chance.

"All right," Ash said finally. "Let's do it."

They opened a new email account for Jacob Brown's pretend parents, then gave that email address to Van Ness Media. Seconds later, a message appeared in the otherwise empty in-box, alerting Jacob Brown's parents that their son wanted to activate a one-week free trial from the fastest-growing educational software company in America. The email provided a link to the usual terms of service and privacy policy—which were still a reading comprehension nightmare—and a button that said APPROVE.

"All set," Ash said into the camera. "Twelve-year-old Jacob Brown is ready to use the full suite of Van Ness Media software."

"Aaaaand cut," said Brielle. "Good work. Now for the fun part. What is he going to create?"

"We could start with a newsletter," suggested Maya, who was clearly prepared for this part. "Then there are those templates we can use."

Happy to follow Maya's lead, Ash opened Van Ness Publisher and clicked on NEWSLETTER TEMPLATES. An option on the first page jumped out at her. It was dark blue and dotted with specks that looked like stars and galaxies. "Space," she said excitedly. "Jacob Brown can be really into planets and stars and stuff."

The editor shrugged. "I like it."

"I like it too," the camerawoman said. "But maybe we should add one more thing. Something companies would want you to buy, so they can show Jacob ads and coupons for it."

They all sat quietly, thinking, until their thoughts were interrupted by the ring of the doorbell and the sound of Brielle's mom calling to them from downstairs. "Girls! Pizza!"

So it was settled. Jacob Brown would fill his Van Ness Media account with stuff about space . . . and pizza.

THE PLANET PIZZA MONTHLY

A newsletter about space and pizza
Editor in chief: Jacob Brown

Cool things about Saturn's rings

Facts from spaceplace.nasa.gov

Saturn's rings are about 240,000 miles wide! That's the distance from the Earth to the moon! They are not solid, though. They're made of particles that scientists think are like icy snowballs. Some of the particles are too small to see and some are as big as a school bus. Saturn probably has 500 to 1,000 rings, and there are gaps between them. Saturn is really cool!

Cool things about pizza

People have been eating some type of pizza since ancient times in Egypt, Greece, and Rome. Pizza with tomato sauce and cheese started as a fast and easy food for poor people in Naples, Italy, in the 1700s and 1800s. Italian immigrants brought pizza to America in the 1900s. It became a popular American food before it became popular in all of Italy. Pizza is yummy and delicious!

It's Not Fair

A haiku by Pluto

I just can't believe
I used to be a planet
But now I am not.

It's Not Fair

A haiku by Jacob Brown

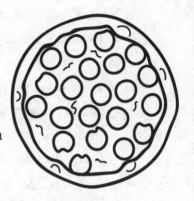

For some reason I'm
Not allowed to have pizza
For three meals a day.

Horoscopes

Aries: Today's a good day for pepperoni.

Taurus: Go ahead, ask for extra cheese.

Gemini: Mercury is in retrograde. Your crust will be soggy.

Cancer: Your pizza will take over an hour to be delivered, but it will be worth it.

Leo: Take a risk and try a new pizza topping. You won't regret it.

Virgo: A bubble in your crust is a sign of good luck.

Libra: Invite a friend over for pizza.

Scorpio: Grounded? Make homemade pizza!

Sagittarius: Be patient or you'll burn that spot on the roof of your mouth right behind your top front teeth.

Capricorn: Stop and smell the pizza.

Aquarius: Mercury is in retrograde. Your favorite pizza place is closed.

Pisces: I see deep dish in your future.

About the editor in chief:

Jacob Brown loves space and pizza. His favorite planet is Jupiter. His favorite star is Rigel. His favorite type of pizza is pepperoni.

CHAPTER 19

Siblings Good Test Subjects for Theory

That night after dinner, while the Simon-Hockheimers were working on a five-hundred-piece puzzle (except for Beckett, who was in his jumper so he couldn't eat the pieces), Ash got a text from Maya.

How long do you think it will take for Jacob Brown to start seeing targeted ads?

"Are you working on the teeth?" Dad asked.

"Huh?" said Ash.

"The shark teeth," Dad repeated. "I have some pieces for you."

"Oh," Ash said. "Yeah. I'll take them." She took the pieces, but she couldn't focus on fitting them into her part of the puzzle. She was thinking about Maya's question. The grocery store had sent Brielle's grandfather a yogurt coupon almost instantaneously, but Dev might wait a few weeks to email his customers about a new study guide. How quickly did Van Ness Media make profiles for their users, and how often did they share those profiles with data brokers or advertisers?

I don't know, she typed back to Maya.

Sadie's head popped up behind Ash's. "What don't you know?" she asked.

"Sadie!" Ash cried, putting her phone screen down on the table. "This is a private conversation."

"Is it about *The Underground News*?" Sadie asked.

"None of your business."

"It is if it's about *The Underground News*. I'm your Story Scout."

"It's still none of your own business."

"Is it about school?"

"Sadie," said Abba in a warning voice. But he was paying more attention to the puzzle. "I finished one eye!" he announced, sliding a bunch of pieces into place.

"Nice," said Dad, giving him a high five.

Maya texted again. *And how will we know if there are ads anyway? Jacob Brown doesn't have a phone.*

"Who's Jacob Brown?" Sadie asked.

"Dad!" Ash cried, covering the screen with her hand. "Sadie's reading my private messages."

"She's sitting right next to me," Sadie said.

"That doesn't mean you have to look," Ash said.

"I can't do a puzzle with my eyes closed!" Sadie closed her eyes and tried to put puzzle pieces together, making a big show of how impossible it was.

Ash closed her own eyes in frustration. "I'm not talking

about looking at the puzzle. I'm talking about looking at my phone."

"Your phone is right by the puzzle."

"That doesn't mean you have to look at it!"

"Girls," said Abba with a sigh. "Does either of you have any fin?"

"Fin!" shouted Beckett from his jumper.

Ash's phone vibrated again. Sadie smiled expectantly. Ash glared at her. Without looking away, she slid her phone, screen down, along the table and pressed it against her leg. Then she got up and walked briskly down the length of their row house to the kitchen. Only once she was at the table with her back to the faraway living room did she turn her phone over to see Maya's next message.

The ads usually come up in a Google search, but we can't do any searches as Jacob Brown. We have to make sure advertisers ONLY know about him from what he puts in Van Ness Media.

Ash took a deep breath and considered this. Maya was right; it was important that Jacob Brown and his interests only appear in Van Ness Media. They'd been careful about this earlier, looking up their Saturn and pizza facts from Brielle's phone instead of "Jacob's" laptop. But Maya had a point now—she was clearly putting a lot of thought into this investigation. If they couldn't search the internet or get phone notifications, how would they know if their test was working?

Sadie's head popped up from around the refrigerator. "Is Jacob Brown your boyfriend?"

"Sadie!" Ash screeched. "Privacy!"

Sadie cracked up and ran back to the living room. But Ash wasn't taking any chances. She took her phone, stomped up the stairs to her room, and closed the door. But it was no use. She was too worked up to concentrate on Maya's questions now.

Bring the laptop tomorrow, she texted. *We can brainstorm at my house after school.*

The bedroom door opened, and Beckett toddled in in his footed fleece pj's. "Jay Brow," he said.

Ash could hear Sadie giggling in the hallway. It wasn't enough for her sister to be annoying, she had to take their baby brother out of his jumper and bring him upstairs, just so he could be annoying too. Ash opened her mouth to scream for her dads, then stopped herself. She had a better idea. One that would test how quickly fake information could travel.

"Come here, Baby Beck," Ash said, pulling him onto the bed and into a snuggle. He still smelled soapy fresh from his bath. "Sadie's in love with a boy named Jacob Brown," Ash whispered in his ear.

"Jay Brow," Beckett said.

"Yes," Ash said. "Sadie loves him. She wants to kiss him!"

"Kiss Jay Brow," Beckett said.

"Right," Ash said. But how reliable was a messenger who couldn't yet speak in full sentences? "Hang on." She sat Beckett on the floor and got a notebook and pen from her backpack. *Dear Sadie,* she wrote. *Thanks for your note. I love you too! Meet me by the big slide at recess tomorrow. Love, your boyfriend, Jacob Brown.*

Just to drive the point home, she wrote *SSH + JB FOREVER* inside a big heart. She folded the paper and scribbled *TOP SECRET, FOR SADIE'S EYES ONLY!!* on the front. Then she handed it to Beckett and whispered, "For Sadie."

Beckett took off down the hall, and Ash went calmly back downstairs to work on the puzzle while she waited.

She didn't have to wait long.

"Ashley!" Sadie screamed from the top of the steps. "Jacob Brown is *not* my boyfriend!"

Their dads looked up from the shark puzzle with raised eyebrows. Ash just smiled and fit together two more pointy teeth. If Van Ness Media was anything like her siblings, they wouldn't be able to keep personal information private for long.

CHAPTER 20

THIS JUST IN:
Proof

The next day after school, Ash and Maya turned on "Jacob's" laptop in their basement television studio. They connected to Wi-Fi and logged in to their fake account. The *Planet Pizza Monthly* was there, just as they'd left it.

"No ads here," Maya said with a frown.

"We knew there wouldn't be, though," Ash pointed out. "There are no ads in Van Ness Media."

"I know they're keeping profiles on all of us. I just know it."

"But how can we prove it if we never leave Van Ness Media?"

Maya placed the laptop on the washing machine and leaned against the dryer. Ash sat down on a step. They both stared at the dusty floor.

"What other information did we give them about Jacob," Maya asked, "when we opened the account?"

Ash thought back to yesterday afternoon, smiling at

the memory of naming too many presidents. "Name, username and password, birthday, email . . ."

Maya stood up straight, her head barely missing the low ceiling. "Maybe there's something in his email?"

Ash shrugged. "It's worth checking. Here, take my phone."

Maya positioned herself for optimum light. Ash brought the laptop to the step. They both waited until a truck passed on the street outside, making a racket and rattling the walls.

"One day has passed," Ash said to the camera, "and it's time to check Jacob Brown's email account." She typed in his username and password, holding a hopeful breath. Then she let it out. "No new emails," she reported, spinning the laptop to face the camera.

Maya cut recording and plopped down next to Ash again, newly disappointed.

"It's only been one day," Ash reasoned. "It might take a lot longer for the information to travel."

"It might even be years," Maya said sadly, like she'd been hoping to avoid sharing this bad news. "Because we're kids. Dev said there are probably companies compiling information about kids, making the profiles more and more detailed, so they can sell them for a real lot of money when we turn eighteen."

Eighteen! Ash thought. Jacob Brown was twelve. "You

mean we might not be able to report on this story for *six years*? Would we have to keep making *Planet Pizza* news-letters every month?"

The videographer rested her head in her hand. "How could we? There are only eight planets."

"And only so many pizza toppings. Or good ones, at least."

Maya giggled. "We'd have to do a whole edition about mushrooms."

Ash put on her news anchor voice. "Jacob Brown here, with everything you ever wanted to know about red peppers."

"Next month," Maya added jokingly, "green."

Ash snorted. "And what will *The Underground News* report on in the meantime? Dog poo?"

Maya wrinkled her nose. "Six years of dog poo on the sidewalk? There'd be nowhere safe to step."

Ash pushed that disgusting thought from her mind and turned the laptop back to face herself. "It's been two minutes. Maybe Jacob got an email now."

"An email about anchovies," Maya joked.

Ash refreshed the page, and they both looked at it expectantly. But apart from the "Welcome to your Van Ness Media free trial" message from yesterday, the in-box remained empty.

"Wait," Ash said. "Look."

It had taken a few seconds to load, but an ad had appeared on the side of the in-box. An ad for . . . Domino's Pizza.

The girls pulled their eyes away from the ad in order to stare at each other.

"Holy moly," Maya whispered. She fumbled for Ash's phone and started recording the screen.

"It could be a coincidence," Ash said, too tingly with nerves and excitement and fear to remember to sound like a newscaster.

She refreshed the page. A new ad loaded. This time, Maya captured her shocked expression first, then slowly panned to reveal the ad: Pizza Hut.

"One more time," Maya mouthed.

Ash hit refresh. The ad reloaded. The Baltimore Planetarium.

Back in news anchor mode, Ash gulped and faced the camera. The Renegade Reporters had hit on a major, major story. "This is Ashley Simon-Hockheimer," she said, "with proof that nothing kids do in Van Ness Media software is private."

CHAPTER 21

Anchors Reflect on Alphabet of Woe

It was tempting to go to air immediately, using only the evidence and footage they had so far. But Brielle said great editing couldn't be rushed, and Maya said they should interview an expert on data brokers, and Ash knew a responsible journalist had to at least ask Van Ness Media for a comment. So, using what they'd learned from Ms. Sullivan, they made a list of everything they'd need to complete their report. It was going to take at least a week to check everything off, which meant Harry had some time to catch up, but Ash tried not to panic. If she went to air now with only half the story, she'd open the door to Harry breaking the rest, like he had with Lucy's bike.

The delay still tested Ash's patience, though, especially because she had to take a one-day break from the investigation to observe a holiday called Yom Kippur. Yom Kippur was the holiest day of the year for Jews, and in Ash's family, that meant refraining from doing any type of work. Ash didn't think Yom Kippur could be called a holiday at all, because it wasn't a happy celebration filled with parties and food; it was a serious day of prayer and reflection. In addition to staying home from work, grown-ups were supposed to fast, which meant Dad and Abba both went twenty-four hours without eating or drinking anything at all, even water. Since Ash wasn't yet thirteen, she didn't need to fast, but she decided that she'd try it this year, as a challenge.

She was challenged from the moment she opened her bedroom door in the morning. The sweet smell of pancakes was drifting up from the kitchen. "Sadie!" Ash said when she saw Abba standing by the stove. "Can't you just have cereal or something?"

"Beckett wants pancakes too," Sadie said, getting the syrup from the refrigerator.

Beckett squealed in his high chair. "An-cake!"

"But Abba's fasting. How do you think he feels making you fluffy, delicious pancakes when he's not allowed to eat them?"

"He didn't really mind," Abba said about himself, pouring batter onto the griddle, "until you talked about how fluffy and delicious they're going to be."

"Sorry, Abba," Ash said.

"I forgive you," Abba said.

Dad came into the kitchen, straightening his tie. "Apologies, forgiveness. You two are really embracing the Yom Kippur spirit."

Yom Kippur was meant to be a day of reflecting on things you did wrong over the past year and thinking about how you could be a better person moving forward. But it was only nine o'clock in the morning, and Ash already wondered how grown-ups thought about anything other than food. She'd planned on fasting at least until lunchtime, when they got back from synagogue. But that was before she'd known there'd be pancakes for breakfast. Sadie was rolling one up and dipping it in syrup.

"You don't have to fast this year," Dad reminded Ash, seeing her staring.

"I know," Ash said with sigh. "But I want to try."

"Yum," said Sadie. A line of syrup dripped slowly down her chin.

Dad rolled his eyes. "And *you* don't have to taunt your sister."

"I'm sorry," Sadie chirped.

"I forgive you," Ash muttered. Then she went back upstairs to get ready for synagogue, hoping she wouldn't be able to smell the pancakes from the shower.

Ash had planned on staying with her parents and grandparents in the adult service this year—she wasn't working or eating, so why not go grown-up all the way?—but Sadie didn't want to go to the kids' service by herself. She spent most of the car ride begging Ash to stay with her, just one more year, and Ash, lacking the willpower to argue without any breakfast in her belly, eventually caved. She regretted it the minute she walked into the kids' service and saw—of course—Harry E. Levin.

"Hi, Ash," he said. "Are you fasting?"

"Trying to. What about you?"

"Yep. I did it last year too. It's easy. I could have gone two whole days if I had to."

It took all of Ash's good Yom Kippur intentions to resist rolling her eyes. She didn't believe him for a second. Leave it to Harry E. Levin to lie and brag on the holiest day of the year.

Sadie wanted to sit in the very front, and Ash didn't argue, figuring Harry wouldn't want to follow. But he did, and he sat down right next to them, even though there were rows of open seats farther back.

"I've been watching your show," he said to Ash.

"Did you watch the episode with Maya's brother?" Sadie asked. "Wasn't it good?"

"Yeah," Harry said judiciously. "It was pretty good."

Ash eyed him suspiciously. "For real?"

He looked right back at her, poker-faced. "For real."

The two of them kept staring at each other, silent. It was such an unexpected way for the conversation to go, neither one seemed to know what to say next.

Sadie chatted on, oblivious to the weirdness. "*The Underground News* is working on a big, top secret story right now. Ash won't tell me what it is, but I think it has to do with Van Ness Media."

"A big, top secret story about Van Ness Media," Harry repeated, his eyes still on his rival anchor. "I'm working on one too."

"You are?" Sadie asked. "For what?"

"*The News at Nine,*" Harry said.

"Whoa!" said Sadie. "I wonder if it's the same news."

Harry gave a mysterious smirk. Ash tried to think of a way to get him to say more without revealing anything herself, but before she could come up with anything, Rabbi Werner approached the podium and clapped her hands.

"Welcome to junior congregation," the rabbi said. "We're going to start with an alphabet game."

Sadie got excited, but Ash sighed. She was too old for alphabet games. Why did she let Sadie talk her into coming to the kids' service?

"On Yom Kippur," the rabbi continued, "we reflect on mistakes we made this past year. We even sing a prayer called the Ashamnu, in which we list our sins alphabetically. So this morning, I'd like us to come up with our own Ashamnu, with a transgression for each letter of the alphabet. I'll begin." The rabbi held up a paper with the letter *A* and said, "For *A*, we could say 'arrogance,' which means acting like you're better than other people." She wrote *arrogance* on the paper, and Ash tried hard not to look at Harry, even though his photo could be in the dictionary under that very word.

"Does anyone else have an *A*?" the rabbi asked.

A boy raised his hand. "Being annoying."

"That starts with a *B*," said his younger brother.

"Now you're just being annoying," the older brother said, and everyone laughed.

"Let's do *B*," said Rabbi Werner.

"Bad behavior?" suggested a girl.

The rabbi wrote it on the *B* paper.

Harry raised his hand. "Bragging," he said.

Easy for you to think of that one, Ash thought.

"Very good," said the rabbi. "*C*?"

"Comparing," Sadie said, "and competing!"

Harry's guilty of those too, Ash thought. So far, he embodied transgressions for every letter of the alphabet.

The game continued. Ash didn't raise her hand at all, but she did come up with words in her head. It was easy since she was sitting next to Harry; all she had to do was think of his personality traits.

"How about *J*?" asked the rabbi.

"Jealousy," Harry said.

He didn't look at Ash as he said it, but she could feel that it was meant for her, and her face got warm with embarrassment. Yes, she'd been jealous of him. So what? It didn't mean she was a bad person. She raised her hand for the first time. The rabbi was quick to call on her. "Judging other people," Ash said pointedly.

"Good one," Rabbi Werner said, writing it down. "*K*?"

"Killing!" shouted a girl in the back.

"Oh my," said the rabbi. "What about *L*?"

"Lying," said Sadie.

"Good one, Sade," Ash whispered. She thought of Harry again, but then her mind drifted to Maria Van Ness. The software CEO claimed she didn't want to expose kids to advertising, but Ash knew she was lying. Maybe it wasn't *technically* a lie, since she didn't have ads in her own software, but she was being very . . .

"Misleading," Ash said for *M*, deciding that maybe she wasn't too old for alphabet games after all. She waited patiently for *P*, then shot her hand into the air to say "Privacy. Well, not respecting someone's privacy."

"Prying?" Harry suggested.

"Sort of," Ash said, but she was drowned out by a girl shouting "Poisoning someone!" It was the same girl who'd said "killing" and "murdering," which meant Rabbi Werner was now looking a bit worried. She hurried the game along until they came up with something for *Z*, "popping zits."

"Great job," the rabbi said. "We've completed an entire Ashamnu, an alphabet of woe. We use the word *we* when reciting the Ashamnu, because even if you, individually, haven't committed a particular sin this past year, someone among us has."

"You mean someone in this room murdered someone with poison?" the girl in the back asked excitedly.

"I hope not," the rabbi said, clearly planning to speak

with the girl's parents later. "But we all make mistakes. And we all need to be able to acknowledge our mistakes so we can apologize, forgive, and resolve to be better. So, what I'd like you all to do now is come up here, walk around, and read the words for every letter. As you do, I want you to silently, privately, think about which of these mistakes *you* might have made this year. When you recognize a mistake you made—and we have all made mistakes—ask yourself, who might your mistake have hurt?"

Sadie jumped up, but Ash was slow to follow. Her empty stomach was grumbling, and the rabbi's words were echoing in her head. It had been fun coming up with words for the bad things the people around her were doing. It was less fun acknowledging what she, herself, had done wrong.

Ash saw Harry pause by the C paper, the one with *comparing* and *competing,* and Ash admitted—silently, privately—that she'd done that as well. (She was doing it right now, she realized, by noticing what he was looking at.) She'd been jealous too, of course. And judgmental. But that had all started when she'd gotten kicked off *The News at Nine.* If she'd been able to stay on the show, Harry never would have become lead anchor, which meant he wouldn't have gotten such a big head, and she wouldn't have had any cause to be jealous and judgmental. That meant it was all Ms. Sullivan's fault, since she was the one who'd kicked her off the show.

Ash sighed, thinking of a new entry for the letter *B*: blaming others. Ms. Sullivan wouldn't have kicked her off the show if it hadn't been for the dancing gym teacher video. And the dancing gym teacher video was Ash's fault. Even if it had been an accident, it wasn't a harmless one. Coach Kelly had been in her office, a place she thought was private. It was kind of like Ash looking at "pre-teen necessities" online. It was humiliating to think that companies might know she *looked* at underwear, while Coach Kelly had two million people watch her dance around in it. Ash felt a pang in her stomach, and she wasn't sure if it was due to hunger this time.

"One last thing before we move on with our service," Rabbi Werner said. "Acknowledging the mistakes we've made is only the first step. The next, very important step is apologizing to the people we've hurt. I know that it can be difficult to say you're sorry out loud, so I invite you all to take a piece of paper and a crayon, and apologize in writing."

About thirty seconds later, Sadie handed Ash a paper on which she'd drawn a flower and scribbled, *Sorry I annoyed you.* Ash smiled and wrote her own card that said, *Sorry I annoyed you too.*

Then, to her surprise, Harry tapped her on the shoulder with a folded piece of paper. It said, *Sorry I bragged about "Young Creatives to Watch."*

Ash blinked at the note. She'd once read a story about a guy who got lost in the desert without anything to eat or drink. After a few days, he started to lose his sanity and thought he saw things that weren't really there. Ash had only skipped one meal, but could the same thing be happening to her? It seemed crazy, but was it any more crazy than Harry handing her an apology note?

In a daze, Ash turned the paper over and wrote, *Sorry I was jealous of you being lead anchor.*

"It's okay," Harry said. He scribbled another note on the paper and handed it back. *Sorry I'm going to break the Van Ness Media story before you.*

Ash burst out laughing, relieved to see the universe restored to its normal state. *Sorry,* she wrote, *but you don't stand a chance.*

"Seriously, though," Harry said. "I'm really close."

"Good job, everyone," said Rabbi Werner. "Please return to your seats. Remember, though, that you can continue to say you're sorry in any way you'd like, once this service is over."

As Ash sat down, she tried not to think about Harry and instead focus on how to apologize—really apologize—to Coach Kelly. She decided that she was going to write her a note once she got home. But first, she was going to have something to eat.

CHAPTER 22

Error Message Derails Plans

If the dots on the Van Ness Media map were tracking the Renegade Reporters' movements over the week, they were recording an impressive example of how to do investigative journalism. The girls traveled around the city asking various kids and parents how they felt about online privacy. They went to the University of Baltimore to interview an expert on data brokers. And they spent lots of time in their basement studio, writing their report, recording takes, and sending emails to various departments at Van Ness Media requesting interviews but never getting a reply.

Just when they were *this close* to finishing the episode, however, things started to go wrong. On Friday afternoon, Brielle got an error message in Movie Maker. She tried to fix it by logging out and closing the browser, but when she went to log back in, Van Ness Media said she had to contact the network administrator. Since her account was through school, she couldn't do anything about it until Monday, when she could talk to her teacher. Luckily, she'd downloaded a rough edit shortly before the error, so she didn't lose all her hard work. But they'd been hoping to go to air by Sunday, and now the episode wouldn't be ready. A whole weekend wasted.

When Monday came, they got more bad news. "Ms. Chung said they have to contact tech support at Van Ness Media," Brielle said at recess. "Which might take a few days."

"A few *days*?" Ash groaned. Now that their reporting was complete, every hour already felt like a day. The days would be like years—years in which Harry E. Levin could make good on his threat.

"She kept asking if I forgot my password," Brielle complained, "but I didn't. Like I'd forget something like that," she scoffed. "But she said that's the only reason anyone's ever had to reset their Van Ness Media password in the middle of the year before."

"You guys," Maya said quietly, "do you think Van Ness Media is onto us? Brielle put everything in Movie Maker, and we've been emailing asking for interviews, so they know what we know. They could be trying to stop us from reporting."

Goose bumps rose on Ash's arms. Could Brielle's error messages and password problems be purposeful?

"The timing must be a coincidence," Ash said uneasily.

"Like we used to think the ads were a coincidence?" Maya said, raising one eyebrow.

Brielle sighed. "No offense, Maya, but you've been totally

paranoid since we started this thing. You guys recorded so much footage, it probably just overloaded the system. I've been working some magic with it, though. This episode is definitely one for my BSA application."

Maya looked like she wanted to say something else, but instead she motioned for them all to be quiet. Harry was walking across the field and right to their group. "Hello," he said cheerily, holding out a tightly folded piece of paper. Ash took it.

From one anchor to another, it said on the outside.

"Goodbye," Harry said. He smiled, turned around, and walked back across the field.

Ash unfolded the note. Then everything dropped: the note, her jaw, her shoulders, her heart, her spirits. "He's going to break the Van Ness Media story tomorrow morning."

"What?" said Maya, picking up the note. "How—how—"

"Did you know about this?" Ash asked Brielle miserably.

"Ouch. Of course not. I'd have told you guys."

Ash collapsed into the grass and closed her eyes. "It's not fair. If it weren't for all those Movie Maker errors, we'd have our episode out by now."

"They're trying to silence us," Maya said, sinking into the grass next to Ash. "I know it."

"Give it a *rest*, Maya," said Brielle, looking down on

them with crossed arms. "If anything, this proves the errors *weren't* on purpose. Why would they be trying to silence *us* and not *The News at Nine*?"

Ash opened her eyes with a flicker of hope. "Maybe Harry's story is different."

Brielle pointed at her. "Yes!" she said excitedly. "Then we can still run our story."

"It's got to be the same news," Maya said, shaking her head. "What other big story about Van Ness Media could there be?"

"Oh, I don't know," Brielle said. "Maybe something about . . . um . . . *anything*?"

Ash was still weighed down with dread, but she forced herself to sit up. "Let us know what you find out after school?" she asked Brielle.

Brielle promised. But all she could let them know was that Harry didn't go to the after-school meeting. According to Ms. Sullivan, he had a dentist appointment. Even worse, Ms. Sullivan wouldn't reveal what his big story was going to be. *All the script says is "Breaking news: Van Ness Media,"* Brielle texted. And *"video clip of Maria Van Ness."*

That made Ash and Maya collapse again, this time onto the linoleum floor of Ash's basement. Harry didn't just have the story, he had a video clip of Maria Van Ness to back it up. And he was going to report it all tomorrow morning, with extra-sparkly teeth.

CHAPTER 23

Breaking News from Van Ness Media

"Good morning, John Dos Passos Elementary. Today is Tuesday, October twenty-second. The cold lunch is tuna salad with crackers. The hot lunch is meatball sub. I'm Harry E. Levin."

"I'm Damion Skinner. And you're watching . . ."

"The News at Nine."

In her classroom, Ash rose onto her tingling legs for the Pledge of Allegiance. After that came the birthdays, then an update from the principal. The wait was excruciating. Who cared about new mulch on the playground when Van Ness Media was about to be exposed for spying on everyone in the school?

Finally, after what felt like hours, Harry said, "And now, breaking news about our sponsor, Baltimore-based Van Ness Media. Van Ness Media sponsors this show and makes many of the applications we use in school every day. But they are also the fastest-growing educational software company in the United States."

Ash's heart was racing, but her ears seemed to be

dragging. Was Harry reading in slow motion? He still wasn't the most natural anchor, but he was acting even more awkward than usual. He sounded like the teacher had called on him to read aloud in class, and he didn't know what any of the words meant.

"Because the CEO of Van Ness Media, Maria Van Ness, lives in Federal Hill herself, she has decided to make a big announcement right here on *The News at Nine*."

Ash glanced at Maya, whose face betrayed the same combination of confusion and hope that Ash felt. So far, Harry didn't have any original reporting. And if Maria Van Ness herself was going to make a big announcement, it couldn't possibly be about something she didn't want people to know. *The Underground News* anchor chanced a smile at her camerawoman and tried to send a telepathic message: *Harry's news is not our news.* But what was it?

The screen filled with a shot of Maria Van Ness sitting on a fancy chair in the Harbor East headquarters. A Van Ness Media sign was behind her. "Hello, John Dos Passos Elementary. I'm Maria Van Ness, founder and CEO of Van Ness Media. My company and I work hard to create software so kids like you can create shows like *The News at Nine*. But we know that creating is a process, and not everyone is ready to share what's in their imagination right away. That's why we're launching a new program called Van Ness Dream Journal."

The video cut to a demonstration of the new program. It

was a cross between a number of other Van Ness applications, with what looked like an empty sheet of notebook paper in the center of the screen. The "paper" filled with squiggles, text, sounds, and photos while Maria Van Ness's voice continued in the background. "Van Ness Dream Journal is a place for you to brainstorm, daydream, and doodle. You can use it for the earliest stages of a school assignment, when the possibilities are wide-open. You can use it to experiment with an idea before transferring it to Writer, Movie Maker, or Art Studio. Or you can use it as a safe, special place for your zaniest dreams, your wildest emotions, and your most personal, private thoughts."

Ash was having pretty wild emotions right now. If she was hearing correctly, Maria Van Ness was encouraging kids to put their most personal, private thoughts and feelings into her software, without telling them that those personal, private thoughts—and exactly where you were standing when you had them—would also be shared with data brokers and advertisers. It was a dream, all right—a dream for the companies making money on private data!

"But that's not all." The CEO was back on the screen. "Because I recently moved to Federal Hill myself, I want *you* to be my beta users. That means John Dos Passos Elementary will get to use Van Ness Dream Journal first, before any other kids at any other schools. After two weeks, we'll ask you to fill out a survey telling us how we could make the program better. We'll incorporate your feedback before we launch Van Ness Dream Journal to the more than five thousand school districts that have contracts with Van Ness Media throughout the United States. That's over ten *million* kids who are counting on *you* to make sure Van Ness Dream Journal is their go-to place for their doodles, daydreams, and ideas. Are you up for the challenge?"

"Yeah!" shouted a few kids in Ash's class. Then they all started talking so excitedly that Mr. Brooks had to clap his hands to calm them down. Ash couldn't hear the end of the announcement over the noise, but that was okay. She understood what was going on far too clearly. It wasn't enough for Maria Van Ness to collect and save kids' movements, or all the details they put in their projects and homework. She also wanted to know their deepest, most personal thoughts, to really flesh out their profiles for advertisers and anyone else who'd pay for the information. The kids at John Dos Passos Elementary were so excited to do it, they were cheering! It wasn't their fault. Maria Van Ness had just told them that Van Ness Dream Journal was a safe place for private thoughts. How could they know it was the exact opposite?

They couldn't, unless someone reported on it.

The News at Nine cut back to Harry, who was beaming from ear to ear. "That was a special announcement with breaking news from Maria Van Ness herself, brought to you *exclusively* by *The News at Nine.* I hope you're all up to the challenge. There are ten million kids throughout the country counting on us."

Ash took a deep breath. Those ten million kids didn't realize it yet, but they were counting on the Renegade Reporters too.

CHAPTER 24

Reporters Weigh Options, Take a Stand

"I did warn you," Harry said in the lunch line, "that I'd break the news first."

Ash pretended to be disappointed. She wanted to get some information of her own before bursting his bubble. "How'd you get the exclusive?" she asked.

"I just called them up!" he said proudly. "I said I was from the show they sponsor at John Dos Passos and we'd heard rumors about something big going on at Van Ness Media, so we wanted to report on it." Harry took his meatball sub and slid his tray down the line. "It was easy, actually. I started with the person who wrote about me for that feature, and he put me right through to someone in public relations. That person asked me a bunch of questions about *The News at Nine* and decided it'd be the perfect place to air their big announcement."

Ash examined the bowl of bananas to find the least spotted one while she considered Harry's methods. Instead of trying to figure out what Ash and her friends were investigating on his own, he'd called Van Ness Media and tried to get them to offer it up. It was a smart approach, actually. No wonder that when Van Ness Media *did* offer something—the launch of Van Ness Dream Journal—he'd run with it, assuming it was what Ash had been investigating all along.

"To be honest," Harry continued, "I was just hoping to break the story. It was pure luck that they offered me an exclusive interview."

"Announcement," Ash corrected.

"What?"

"It wasn't an *interview*. You didn't sit down with Maria Van Ness and ask her questions. She just recorded a video of herself for *The News* to air."

"It's okay," Harry said, patting her hand. "You're allowed to be jealous this time. I don't know how you couldn't be." He tossed an apple in the air, caught it, and placed it on his tray. Then he walked back to his table, where his friends were fighting over who got to sit next to him. Ash looked away quickly, not wanting to lose her appetite, and took her usual seat.

"Well," Brielle said when she arrived, "he didn't steal our story."

"No," said Maya, seething. "But Van Ness Media is about to steal the private thoughts of ten million kids all over America." Her arms were crossed over her chest, and she hadn't even opened her lunchbox.

"We've got to get our report out," Ash said, "right away."

But Brielle shook her head. "I don't know if we can go to air now."

"You saved a rough version somewhere before you got the error, right?" Ash asked her. "You can upload that to my account and finish editing tonight. I'll give you my password."

"It's not that," Brielle said. "It's the timing. Our news seems sort of dead on arrival."

Maya looked confused. "What do you mean? It's more alive than ever. More *important* than ever."

"Van Ness Media sponsors our school news show," Brielle explained. "Maria Van Ness made a special video just for our school. They're letting us be the beta users for Van Ness Dream Journal. Everyone's super excited. If we go reporting bad news about them, how do you think it will look?"

Maya gaped at her. "Truthful?" she tried.

"Maya's right," Ash said, determinedly peeling her semi-spotted banana. "We have to report it. All these people think what they put in this new program is private. But it's not. Don't you think they have a right to know?"

"Honestly?" Brielle said with a frown. "I don't think people care."

"They'd care if they knew!" Maya cried.

Brielle shrugged. "Probably not. Google and TikTok and Instagram and *YouTube*, which *our* show is on—they're all collecting and selling information about everyone, and nothing changes because nobody really cares. What will happen if we go live with our news?" Maya opened her mouth to respond, but Brielle cut her off with "What will *really* happen, Maya? Will people stop using Van Ness Media? Probably not. Will the three of us get in trouble? One hundred percent."

Ash hadn't considered it that way. It felt like Brielle had thrown cold water at her. "We got kicked off *The News at Nine* because the dancing gym teacher video made Van Ness Media look bad," she said nervously. "And this makes Van Ness Media look much worse."

"If I get kicked off *The News at Nine*," Brielle added, "I might as well rip up my BSA application, and there goes my filmmaking career."

Maya looked like she was about to cry. But she didn't. She sat up straighter and spoke firmly, looking Brielle right in the eye. "What's the point of becoming a film-maker if you're not going to make videos that matter? And maybe you're right, and people won't care, but they at least have a right to know what's happening." She took a breath, but she wasn't done. "I'm going to get our report out there somehow, even if I have to record and edit it myself."

Ash stared, speechless, at her best friend. Maya had always been there for her, silent but supportive, holding a camera so that Ash could talk to the world. Now Maya had found something she wanted to say—no, *needed* to say. It was only fair that Ash make sure she could say it.

"I'm with you," Ash said. "We'll probably get in trouble, but we need to do it anyway."

Maya beamed and hugged Ash from the side. They both looked at Brielle.

The editor sighed. She shook her head. But then she said, "All right. I'm with you too." She held out her hands to ward off a hug, adding, "There's no need to get all extra about it."

"Holy moly!" Maya cried, collapsing dramatically onto her lunchbox. "Thank goodness. There's no way I could have done this on my own."

CHAPTER 25

Reporters Report to Principal's Office

Deciding to report the news was one thing. Being able to report it was another. Brielle logged into Maya's Van Ness Media account that night, but when she uploaded what she had of the report, the error messages started again, and it wasn't long until Maya's account was kicked out of the program, just like Brielle's. When Brielle texted what happened, Ash tried to open the Movie Maker app on her phone, but it wouldn't even load. *ACCOUNT ERROR*, the screen said. *CONTACT NETWORK ADMINISTRATOR.*

The girls brought their issues to Ms. Chung first thing the next morning, and Friday, ten minutes before school ended, all three of them were called down to the principal's office. The last time Ash and Maya were in the principal's office was in May, right after the video of Coach Kelly had gone viral, and Ash had known a big punishment was coming. The look on Mr. Carver's face now made it clear that he had not forgotten about what happened last school year, and a punishment might be coming again. Ash didn't know why he'd be angry with them now, but she still got the heavy feeling through her body that she'd gotten in May. It might have even been worse, because Brielle had warned that they'd get in trouble, and here they were, including Brielle.

"Ms. Chung spoke with someone at Van Ness Media today," Mr. Carver said. "According to them, all three of your accounts have been"—he glanced at a Post-it note on his desk—"temporarily suspended for violating the terms of service."

Mr. Carver could have said their accounts had accidentally unleashed an ancient curse, Ash was so shocked and scared. This meant the error messages weren't just a coincidence, and they weren't because the files were too big. It had to be what the files contained.

Was it against the rules to use Van Ness Media to say negative things about Van Ness Media? Did it say that in the terms of service? Ash had no idea, because the terms of service document was just as long and incomprehensible as the privacy policy.

"Given your *history*," Mr. Carver said sternly, looking at Ash and then Maya, "I would have thought you'd know better than to record inappropriate videos again."

"We didn't record anything inappropriate," Ash promised.

"Then why is our educational media provider saying you violated their rules?"

The three girls looked at one another, and Mr. Carver

clearly took that as an admission of guilt. "I know Van Ness programs are fun, but that doesn't mean there are no rules. Students must adhere to their terms of service."

"Do you know what the terms of service say," Ash asked, her reporter instincts taking over, "or who agreed to them?"

"Don't get smart with me, Miss Simon-Hockheimer."

"I'm not—I'm just—" Ash didn't know how to phrase her question without sounding like she was talking back, but she desperately needed to ask it. "Do you know who agreed to the terms of service? Because, um, a friend of mine tried to sign up at home, and an adult had to approve it."

"I—I don't know," the principal said, clearly caught off guard by the question. "Someone from the district head-quarters, I suppose. You'd have to talk to North Avenue." Then he stopped, seeming to remember that he was in charge of this meeting, not Ash. "The point," he said firmly, "is that you must use the software appropriately. I don't know what you put in your Van Ness Media accounts, but it must have been pretty serious to warrant this action. We've never had this happen before in all the years we've been using this software."

Maya started to cry. Ash took her hand, letting the news sink in.

"So," Brielle said quietly, "Van Ness Media decided to shut down our accounts because of what we put in them?"

"Correct," Mr. Carver said. "Ms. Chung will set you up with temporary guest accounts that you can use until this matter is sorted, but you must use them for your school assignments and nothing else. Is that clear?"

Maya was still crying, so Mr. Carver handed her a tissue.

"Van Ness Media knows what we were working on because they're tracking everything we do!" Ash blurted. "*They're* the ones who should be in trouble. They locked us out of our accounts because—"

"Miss Simon-Hockheimer," the principal said sharply, cutting her off. "You are in sixth grade now. It's time to start taking responsibility for your own actions. Last year, you tried to blame the incident with Coach Kelly on everyone but yourself. Now you're trying to blame this on Van Ness Media."

"They're selling our information to advertisers!" Ash said desperately, jumping up.

Ash's team all nodded, but Mr. Carver shook his head. "Van Ness Media software is free of advertising."

"It's true," Brielle pleaded. "If you look at what we were working on, you'll see."

"All of your files are under review at Van Ness Media," the principal replied, "while they decide if you violated the terms of service."

Maya let out a shaky breath.

"They won't let you see what we were working on?" Ash asked, slowly lowering herself back into her chair. She could almost laugh, it was so outrageous.

"I'm not sure I want to, to be frank. They don't think *anyone* should see what you were 'working on,' and I'm sure they have a good reason."

Yeah, Ash thought. *Because they don't want anyone to know what we know. Especially not school principals.*

The bell rang. School was over. Apparently, so was this meeting. Mr. Carver walked to the door and opened it.

"Ms. Chung will have your temporary usernames and passwords tomorrow. If you don't use them appropriately, you will not only be suspended from Van Ness Media. You could be suspended from school."

CHAPTER 26

Surprise Sighting in Park

The Renegade Reporters stood in the middle of the hallway while kids poured past them on their way out of school. It was Friday, which meant Brielle didn't have *The News at Nine*, but now they couldn't work on *The Underground News* either. They walked, zombie-like, to get their backpacks and then outside. Ash texted Olive to say they'd be late, and the three girls wandered silently around the neighborhood until they found themselves at Federal Hill Park.

It was a cool, cloudy day. The wind on the hill only added to their negative energy. The playground was nearly empty, so the three girls sat on the swings, which hung too low for them to actually swing, making it a fitting place to wallow in disillusionment.

"He didn't let us explain," Brielle said. "He didn't even want to look at our video."

"They're spying on us," Maya said, "and they're selling our personal information, and now they're going to stop us from reporting it."

"They say they want kids to create things," Ash said, "but they won't let us create anything important. Are we just supposed to report on stupid stuff like the dog poo bandit?"

They sat in silence for a few minutes, the tops of their shoes scraping the ground and Maya letting out the occasional sniffle. Ash looked at the city skyline. That usually cheered her up, but today the buildings were wrapped in clouds, which made them look as gray as she felt.

A dog appeared on the edge of the playground. It stopped by the fence and barked, making all three girls look up. It was a Saint Bernard, huge and white with a brown patch that made it look like it was wrapped in a blanket. The dog barked again and ran around to the flag pole. Ash felt a jolt of recognition. She'd seen that dog before: in that exact spot, in the photo on the Van Ness Media website. The photo where Maria Van Ness had posed with her own Saint Bernard. And again in Harry's "exclusive" video. The one in which Maria Van Ness announced Van Ness Dream Journal.

"Bernard!" came a woman's voice from behind the fence. "Come here, Bernard."

The dog barked and ran back around. A woman's body rose up over the hill. Her silver hair appeared first. Then her glasses. Her black scarf. Black jacket. Black leggings. Black sneakers.

Ash grabbed her friends' hands and squeezed them hard. There was no mistaking it. The woman was Maria Van Ness.

"Holy moly," Maya whispered. "What do we do?"

"Keep facing this way," Ash whispered back. "Don't let her see our faces."

"Good boy," the CEO said to Bernard. "Go play."

The dog took off around the path, and Maria Van Ness walked up to the fence that surrounded the playground. She leaned against it, not even five feet from the swings, and said, "What a dreary day."

Ash was suddenly consumed with so much anger, she could barely contain it. *Maria Van Ness* was complaining about this day? After what she'd just done to Ash and Maya and Brielle? After what she was doing to all the kids at John Dos Passos and across the country? She thought she had the right to expose what all those kids believed they were doing in private, but the minute someone got close to exposing what *she* was doing in private, she tried to shut them up? Well, she couldn't shut Ash up in real life.

"I'm going to talk to her," Ash declared.

"Are you serious?" Brielle asked.

Ash stood up from her swing.

"Wait!" Maya said. "Give me your phone."

It took a second for Ash to realize what Maya was going to do. Then she looked at Brielle, who nodded. Ash marveled at her friends' bravery. "Here," she said, handing over the phone to the camerawoman.

"Stay close to her, Maya," the director said quietly. "And try to talk loud, Ash, because of the wind."

The anchor nodded, her heart pounding. Maria Van Ness had walked around the path and taken a seat on a bench overlooking Harbor East, her own company's headquarters viewable across the water. She couldn't have asked Maya to set up a better shot.

"Here we go," Ash said. She set purposefully across the grass until she was standing right behind the CEO. Maya got into position and pressed record. Brielle mouthed, "Go."

"Maria Van Ness?" Ash said loudly.

The CEO turned around.

"We're the Renegade Reporters with *The Underground News*. Is the information kids put in Van Ness Media software kept private?"

CHAPTER 27

EXCLUSIVE INTERVIEW:
Maria Van Ness

"Excuse me?" the CEO said.

"You claim you make money by selling software, not your users' attention spans. But our investigation suggests that that's not true. How do you respond?"

Maria Van Ness narrowed her eyes behind her glasses. She looked from Ash to Brielle to Maya to the phone she was holding. "Turn that off, please," Maria Van Ness said.

Maya's lip trembled, but she kept recording.

The CEO rose from the bench and turned to face the news crew. She was tall, and she held her head high and her shoulders back. "Stop recording," she said calmly but firmly. Her tone reminded Ash that before Maria Van Ness became a software mogul, she was a teacher. The anchor realized she could use that information.

"You used to be a teacher," Ash said. "In an interview with CNN, you said that's why you started Van Ness Media, because you saw how much advertising kids were exposed to in educational software, and you thought you could do better."

The CEO raised her eyebrows. She was clearly impressed that Ash had watched her interview. Impressed enough that she seemed to put aside her concern about being recorded. "That's right," Maria Van Ness said. "Advertising was everywhere in those programs. I could see that that was where online software was moving. Parents didn't care about the ads, and kids barely even noticed."

"But you said kids are very susceptible to advertising."

"Oh yes." Maria Van Ness sat down and placed an arm on the back of the bench, settling into the interview. "Developing brains are very impressionable. That's why they're so valuable to advertisers."

"Valuable," Ash repeated. "Like, worth a lot of money."

"Indeed."

Ash took a deep breath. "Is that why Van Ness Media gives kids' information to advertisers?"

"To make money?" Maria Van Ness laughed. "All companies want to make money."

Ash held her breath. It wasn't a confession, but it wasn't a denial either. "Including yours?" she pressed. "You said you could do *better* than those other companies."

"Of course I could," the CEO replied, waving her hand as though shooing away a fly. "The products they were advertising were all wrong. Sugary cereals, toys for the wrong age group. I thought I'd stay out of the whole thing, but I couldn't let such a valuable opportunity go to waste. I *knew* I could do better."

There it was. In all those interviews, Maria Van Ness made it sound like she'd wanted to protect kids from advertising, when she'd actually wanted to expose them to better, *targeted* advertising. And she had just admitted it. She'd confessed to everything they'd accused her of. Ash glanced quickly at her team and knew they'd all heard the same thing.

"But, what about privacy?" Ash asked.

Maria Van Ness's eyes moved from Ash to Brielle to Maya, a look of recognition slowly washing over her. She stood up. "I know who you are. You're that girl with the 'news' show." She used her fingers to make quotes in the air around the word *news*. "Kind of funny to ask *me* about privacy," the businesswoman continued, "when you're a twelve-year-old with her own YouTube channel."

That caught Ash off guard. "That—that's different," she said. "I *choose* what to put on my TV show. I *know* people are going to watch it."

"Aren't you the same girl who recorded that teacher in her underwear?" Maria Van Ness asked, like a teacher leading a discussion about a book. "Did *she* know people were going to watch that? Millions of people?"

Ouch. "That . . . that was a mistake. But you . . ." Ash summoned her nerve and stood up straighter, hoping to mimic the CEO's posture and confidence, but nothing else. "You're lying to people. And you're trying to stop us from telling the truth. The three of us—we all just got locked out of our Van Ness Media accounts for violating the terms of service."

"Well, that's a shame." The CEO frowned, her silver hair blowing in the wind. "I'm not lying to anyone. If you three were using Movie Maker, you agreed to the terms, and to the privacy policy. Not just you, but hundreds of thousands of users, all over the country. It's all written down for everyone to see." She walked around the bench, closer to Ash. "Listen, I make the best digital media software for the education market, hands down. Surely, you agree? I'd like to see you make your little show with a different editing program." She smiled now and leaned against the back of the bench. "Kids use my creations to make things like—what is it?—*The Undercover News*. And I use *their* creations to fund the operation and grow the company. Everyone wins."

Ash was speechless. Maria Van Ness was serious. She truly didn't think she was doing anything bad. In fact, she thought she was doing something good.

"But," Ash said.

The CEO waited, her eyebrows high above the rims of her glasses. "But what?" she said finally. "Privacy? No one cares about privacy. Not if you give them a good product in exchange." She sighed, like she was sad about it. "Some people think they care, but they don't. Not enough to do anything about it. Right? Let's be serious. Do you think your 'investigative reporting' will move people to action?"

The girls stood there, unable to answer.

"That's what I thought." Maria Van Ness took off her glasses and cleaned them on her scarf. "Now, I was going to make you delete this recording you've been taking of me without my permission. But you know what? I don't think I need to bother. Put it on your little show if you want. Who's going to watch it? Who's going to care?" She swung her head back to move her hair from her eyes, then put her glasses back on and stood tall. "Well, I must be going. Bernard!"

The dog came running and barked happily. "Good boy," Maria Van Ness said, petting him and offering him a treat from her pocket. But Bernard didn't take it. He stood very still, concentrating. "Oh, you haven't gone yet?" Maria Van Ness said to him. "Well, hurry it up, then. Do your business."

He did. He was a big dog, and his business made a big pile. The size of the piles that had been left all over the sidewalks of Federal Hill the past few months. The same piles that the girls had narrowly avoided stepping in and had joked about investigating countless times.

"Thanks for the interview," Maria Van Ness said cheerily to the reporters. "And thanks for using Van Ness Media!"

She walked briskly around the path and disappeared down the hill. Bernard trotted after her, his poo still in the park.

CHAPTER 28

ANALYSIS:
Video Evidence Solid

After they got over their initial shock, the team rushed to Brielle's house, which was closest. It was downhill, and the wind was at their backs, so they practically sprinted there.

"Did we get it all?" the anchor asked once they'd raced inside and closed the door. "Please tell me we got it all."

Maya held the phone with sweaty hands. "Four minutes . . ." She pressed play. Both Ash and Maria Van Ness were clearly visible. Their voices were quiet but clear, except for a few short gusts of wind that, thankfully, didn't drown out any of the incriminating evidence.

Ash puffed out a big breath, wiped her forehead with her hand, and sank onto Brielle's couch. She felt like she'd just completed the Baltimore marathon.

Brielle sat next to her. "I can clean up the sound and make it louder," she assured them, panting. "I can even add captions too. I just need to find a way to edit it."

"Well," Maya said, a smile playing at her lips, "Maria

Van Ness said she'd *like* to see us make our show using some other software."

The three girls looked at one another, then burst out laughing. There was something darkly funny about using a competitor's software to bring down Maria Van Ness. And this video would definitely bring her down . . . just as soon as they could bring it to air.

CHAPTER 29

Reporters Seek Approval, Support

That night, as contractually obligated, all three Renegade Reporters planned to share the Van Ness Media story with their permission-granting adults. Brielle still had the rough version of the episode that she'd downloaded before getting locked out of her account, so she emailed that file to the other two, and Ash emailed the video of their encounter with Maria Van Ness in the park.

Ash was anxious to show her parents as soon as possible, but Abba was working late and Dad was busy with the little ones, so the anchor had to wait, jittery with nerves and anticipation, until long past her bedtime.

Finally, with Beckett asleep and Sadie having eventually given up on listening from the stairs, Abba came home, and Dad warmed his dinner, and Ash pressed play, first on the rough edit, then on the new footage. She stood behind them while they watched it, her foot tapping nervously.

When the video ended, Abba gave a low whistle. "This is serious, Ash."

"I know."

"Very thorough reporting," Dad said. "Research, a test case, explanations from experts . . . The hard work shows."

"Thanks. We have to incorporate the footage from the park, and we should probably add something about Van Ness Dream Journal now too, but I'm not sure how we can because we're all locked out of our Van Ness Media accounts." She told him about the error messages and the meeting with the principal and the claim that they'd violated the terms of service. "He wouldn't even listen to us," Ash said. "But maybe he will once our episode goes live, especially now that we have this interview with Maria Van Ness."

"Oh, I'm sure he'll be hearing from a lot of people once word gets out," Abba said. "You kids have to use this software at school, and parents have no idea what's going on."

"How did *you* figure out what's going on?" Dad asked. "I knew you were doing something about Van Ness Media, but I figured it was more . . . neutral."

"Yeah, that was our original plan. But that day we went there, Maya and I . . . um . . ." Ash took a deep breath. "We sort of walked in on a meeting about this stuff. By accident."

Abba widened his eyes and leaned toward her. Dad closed his eyes and shook his head.

"We didn't mean to," Ash went on. "Honest. But they were looking at a map of Federal Hill with little dots on it, and talking about user profiles and tracking locations, and they clearly didn't want us to know what they were doing. I guess we sort of invaded their privacy." Ash gave an awkward smile. "But then we started investigating and found out they've been invading ours."

"I'll say." Dad's face took on a look that Ash couldn't quite read.

Now Abba had the same inscrutable expression as Dad. "Ashley," he said seriously, and Ash felt sure she was in trouble. Again. At least this day had prepared her for it. But to her surprise, Abba's face broke into a smile. "We're very proud of you."

Ash's body was still tense, braced for a punishment. "You are?"

"Yes. It takes real courage to do this sort of work. And it will take real courage for you and your friends to put it on the air."

"But you'll let us?" Ash asked, crossing her fingers on both hands.

Dad glanced at Abba, who nodded. "Absolutely. It's important that you tell people what's going on."

Ash loved her dads so much, she wanted to eat them. She threw herself into their arms for a big hug. "Thank you," she said. This had been a long, emotional day, and it was catching up to her. She felt like she could fall asleep this very moment, now that she knew she had her dads' support. "You're not mad that we barged in on that meeting?" she confirmed, stifling a yawn.

"Some of the biggest discoveries start with pure luck," Abba said.

"But, Ashley," Dad said pointedly, looking his daughter in the eye. "You really need to learn how to knock."

CHAPTER 30

Underground News Aims Beyond Basement

On Monday at lunch, the Renegade Reporters' table was positively buzzing. Brielle's parents had been so proud of her, they'd bought her professional software called Final Cut Pro. She'd downloaded it Friday night and spent the whole weekend editing *The Underground News*. Ash and Maya had spent the weekend in the studio recording Ash's anchor spots, which meant Brielle just needed to add them in, and the Van Ness Media episode would be ready to air.

"Is Final Cut Pro better than Van Ness Movie Maker?" Ash asked.

"It's so slick," Brielle said dreamily. "Our episode is looking amazing."

"Maya's family can't wait to share it with everyone they know," Ash said, elbowing her best friend.

Maya looked down at the table, but she smiled so big, it seemed like rays of sunshine could be radiating from her face. "My mom called Dev to tell him about it. She said, 'Have you heard about your sister, the activist?'"

"I'll stay up all night adding those anchor spots, if I have to," Brielle promised. "The sooner people know what Maria Van Ness is doing, the better. That woman is evil."

Ash didn't think it'd be possible for Maya to look any happier, but somehow, she did. "You mean you don't want companies tracking what you do online anymore?" Maya asked.

Brielle shrugged one shoulder. "I still don't think it's a big deal that they tell advertisers about me," she clarified. "But Maria Van Ness is trying to hide it, so *she* clearly thinks it's bad. And she lets her dog poop all over the sidewalk and doesn't pick it up. The world deserves to know."

The girls laughed. But then Ash got serious. "Do you think what Maria Van Ness said is true?" she asked her friends between bites of fried chicken. "That no one will watch it or care? We don't exactly have a ton of subscribers."

"I was thinking . . ." Maya took a sip of her juice, then continued. "Maybe we can send this episode somewhere bigger. Like one of the Baltimore TV channels, or even CNN."

"They probably wouldn't bother watching our clip, though," Brielle said, "because we're kids."

"We can at least *try*," Maya said. "Unless you can think of a news show with lots of viewers that won't care if we're kids."

Just then, a raucous clatter came from the boys' table. They'd been using their lunch trays like Jenga blocks, and the whole tower had collapsed.

Ash looked at Damion, Khalil, and Harry, then at her team. It pained her to say it, but it was for the greater good. "There is one show that has three hundred viewers every morning," she said. "And I happen to know the lead anchor."

CHAPTER 31

Anchor Offers Exclusive

Harry stared at the screen. He pressed his hands into his eyes, then stared at the screen again. "How'd you get this interview?" he asked.

"She just happened to come to Federal Hill Park while we were there," Ash said.

Harry snorted. "Lucky break."

"I know."

It was Tuesday after school. Brielle had finished the episode the night before, like she'd promised, and everyone agreed it was ready to air.

Brielle had wanted to take it straight to Ms. Sullivan, but Ash knew how important it was for a lead anchor to have control over his or her reporting. If she wanted Harry on board, she needed to go to Harry directly. Even if it meant offering her rival the scoop of a lifetime. So after the bell rang, Ash had stopped Harry in the hall outside their classroom, before he could go to *The News at Nine*.

"Well," Harry said, leaning against the wall, "you

weren't lying. You got the bigger story on Van Ness Media. I guess you win."

"It's not a competition," Ash said.

Harry gave her a look.

"Okay, it is a competition. But no one's winning right now. Except Van Ness Media. They know everything about all of us, and no one knows anything about them."

"Well, you've got proof now," Harry said. "You can report this on your show."

"I can, but not many people watch my show."

"So?"

"The whole school watches yours."

Harry drummed his fingers against the wall, finally catching on. "You're offering me this story?"

Ash nodded. "No one else has seen it yet. I'm offering you the exclusive."

The anchor's eyes widened. "You want me to air this on *The News at Nine*? Which is sponsored by Van Ness Media?"

The other anchor chanced a smile. "They kind of deserve it, don't you think?"

Harry let out a low whistle. "I don't know if Ms. Sullivan will approve it. Or did you want me to do it without telling her?"

Ash was impressed with his nerve, but not with his idea. She knew better than anyone that Ms. Sullivan didn't like surprises on *The News at Nine.* "Don't do that. You don't want to get kicked off the show."

"I doubt she'll let us report it," Harry said, thinking.

Ash held her breath. Harry wanted to do it, she could tell, but he was nervous. Now it was time to seal the deal. If her rival anchor was anything like herself, she knew exactly how. "Just ask her," Ash said casually. "If she says no, we'll take it to CNN."

Sure enough, he took the bait. "You're offering this story to me before *CNN*?" Harry asked incredulously.

Ash shrugged. "For now," she said coolly. "But we can't sit on it forever. How about you let me know by tomorrow?"

But Harry had already decided. "All right," he said. "Let's go talk to Ms. Sullivan."

Yes! Ash thought. She said, "Go ahead. I'll wait here."

"No," Harry said. "You have to come with me."

"You're lead anchor."

"It's your story."

"But I offered it to you."

"It's on *your* phone!" Harry pressed it into her hands, walked to the stairs, and waited. "Come on."

Ash dragged her feet along, her stomach in knots. The last time she'd talked to Ms. Sullivan, it was right after the first *News at Nine* broadcast of the year. When Ms. Sullivan had told her to be a team player or get off the team. For weeks, Ash had been angry at her, furious that a teacher she'd looked up to for so long—the person who'd inspired Ash's love of reporting to begin with—had let her down. But as she forced herself toward the studio now, Ash realized it was the opposite. Ms. Sullivan hadn't let her down; *she'd* let Ms. Sullivan down. First with the Dancing Gym Teacher, and then with her attitude. What had she said back in September? That the show was bad without her, and that since she wasn't lead anchor, she was going to quit? She must have sounded like a spoiled brat. And now here she was, facing Ms. Sullivan for the first time since then—with a negative story about *The News at Nine*'s sponsor. What would Ms. Sullivan think of her now? *I can just quit journalism again,* Ash thought. *That'd be easier than showing my face in the studio.*

But she had major news that she needed Harry to report. It was a wonder he was willing to help her at all—she hadn't exactly been nice to him the past few weeks. The least she could do was swallow her shame and help him help her.

The News at Nine crew was sitting around the big tables, planning their next show. The scene was so familiar, it hit Ash like a gust of wind, almost knocking her over. Ms. Sullivan looked up and saw her. "Hello, Ashley," she said, cautiously friendly, like Ash was a kitten that might scratch.

"Hi," Ash said.

"Ash brought us a story to report," Harry said. "With exclusive footage."

"Is that so?" said Ms. Sullivan, head cocked. "Well, let me see it."

From the corner of the room, Brielle gave Ash a thumbs-up with one hand and a fingers-crossed with the other. Ash handed her phone to Ms. Sullivan, who stepped out into the hallway to watch the video in private. Ash stood in the doorway, staring at Ms. Sullivan's back and praying that she would find the reporting halfway decent.

When the episode ended, the teacher let out a big breath and looked Ash in the eye, her face still unreadable. "Why did you bring this to *The News at Nine*?" she asked.

It felt like a test. Ash gave the truthful answer, hoping it was also correct. "Because my show doesn't have that many subscribers, and I think it's important that people know what's going on."

Ms. Sullivan blinked at her.

"I'm not trying to get revenge or anything," Ash added nervously. "For real. I deserved to be kicked off *The News at Nine*. And Harry's a pretty good anchor. I mean, a very good anchor. The show is very good too. It keeps everyone at school informed. And I really want them to be informed about what Van Ness Media is doing." Then she made herself stop talking and breathe.

Ms. Sullivan handed Ash's phone back to her. "Coach Kelly told me you sent her a very nice note."

"Yeah," Ash said, her face getting warm. "I apologized for invading her privacy."

The corners of Ms. Sullivan's mouth were inching upward. "Do you want to report this on *The News at Nine* yourself?"

One little question, and Ash's heart caught. She felt a physical pull toward the anchor chair. But she resisted it. "Harry's lead anchor," she said. "He should do it."

Ms. Sullivan's lips were now in a full smile. "You made this news episode all by yourself?"

"With Maya and Brielle. We started it using Van Ness Movie Maker."

That made her teacher laugh. Ash laughed too.

"I'm proud of you, Ashley. You're an excellent reporter. But you're an even more excellent person."

Ash couldn't help herself. She rushed up to Ms. Sullivan and wrapped her in a hug. The teacher laughed and hugged her back.

Harry, Damion, and Brielle stuck their heads into the hallway. "Does this mean we're going to run the story?" Brielle asked.

"If the anchors are up to it," Ms. Sullivan said. "It's not very good publicity for our sponsor."

"I stepped in dog poo *twice* last week," Damion said. "Let's make that lady pay."

CHAPTER 32

Breaking News at Nine

"Good morning, John Dos Passos Elementary. Today is Wednesday, October thirtieth. The cold lunch is peanut butter and jelly. The hot lunch is black bean burrito bowl. I'm Harry E. Levin."

"I'm Damion Skinner. And you're watching . . ."

"The News at Nine."

Ash wasn't behind the anchor's desk, and she wasn't in the studio, but she'd never been so nervous for *The News at Nine.*

For the three hundred students and staff members at Johns Dos Passos Elementary, this was an ordinary episode so far. They stood for the Pledge of Allegiance and listened to the birthday report and chuckled at the knock-knock joke of the week. They had no idea what was coming next.

"And now," Harry said, "a special report about our sponsor, Baltimore-based Van Ness Media. This story was investigated by John Dos Passos sixth graders and former

News at Nine crew members, Ashley Simon-Hockheimer and Maya Joshi-Zachariah, with editing by *The News at Nine* director, Brielle Diamond. They brought this story to *The News at Nine* because they thought it was important that we know what's happening in our school."

Mr. Brooks and everyone in the class turned to look at Ash and Maya. Maya hid her head in her hands. Ash kept her face pointed toward the screen. She knew that down the hall, in the studio, Brielle was saying, "*The Underground News* episode in three . . . two . . ."

And there it was, on the screen. Broadcast live into every classroom for every student and every teacher. Later today, it'd be available in the school online portal for any parents or former students who wanted to watch. It'd also be on *The Underground News* YouTube channel for anyone else in the world to see. Her story. Her friends' hard work. Their news. Breaking.

THE UNDERGROUND NEWS, EPISODE 4

REPORTER: Ashley Simon-Hockheimer
VIDEOGRAPHER: Maya Joshi-Zachariah
EDITOR: Brielle Diamond
SLUG: Van Ness Media

VIDEO	AUDIO
Anchor on Camera	**ANC:** Coming up: Shocking news about the fastest-growing educational software company in the country. We're the Renegade Reporters, and you're watching *The Underground News.*
Intro and Credits	NONE
Anchor on Camera	**ANC:** If you're a kid, chances are you've used Van Ness Media software. Maybe you've drawn something in Van Ness Art Studio, or written an essay in Van Ness Writer. Van Ness Media sponsors my school's morning announcements show, *The News at Nine,* which means they provide the software and all the equipment. And until recently, this very show, *The Underground News,* was edited using Van Ness Movie Maker.

Ext. of Van Ness Media Headquarters	**ANC:** Van Ness Media is based here in Baltimore, but the company is growing and growing. According to the founder and chief executive officer, Maria Van Ness, they have contracts with more than five thousand school districts across the United States, which means more than ten million kids in three hundred thousand classrooms use their software.
Anchor on Camera	**ANC:** One of the biggest selling points for schools is privacy. Unlike many other applications, Van Ness Media doesn't allow any advertising inside their software. But that doesn't mean students' personal information is kept private. In fact, *The Underground News* discovered that Van Ness Media is keeping detailed profiles on all of its users, including location data, and giving that information to advertisers . . . and maybe to others as well.

| Corey Fox in his Office | **ANC voiceover:** To get some background, the Renegade Reporters spoke with Corey Fox, a law professor at the University of Baltimore. He specializes in online privacy. |
| Anchor with Corey Fox in Office | **COREY FOX:** The internet is an amazing thing. It lets us find information, go shopping, watch videos, connect with friends, and lots of other things, most of them for free, yeah? But every time you and I do any of those things, we leave a trail of information, called a digital fingerprint. It's kind of like your physical fingerprint, because it's unique to you.

Companies are collecting that information. They keep track of what you and I search for, and what we buy, and, through the GPS on our phones, where we go in real life. If you put all that information together, you can make a very detailed picture of who each user is. That's valuable information.
ANC: What do you mean by valuable?
COREY FOX: Well, I mean a few things. But to start with, it's valuable in a literal sense. It's worth a lot of money.
ANC: Why? |

Anchor with Corey Fox in Office cont.	**COREY FOX:** A lot of reasons. But a big one is advertising. Let's say you look at something online—a book, or a pair of jeans, or the cost of flights to . . . Jamaica. Then you open up the Facebook app. Chances are you'll see ads for that book, or those jeans, or maybe hotels in Jamaica. That's because companies are working together. They're taking information about you and selling it to advertisers.
Footage of Van Ness Media Software	**ANC voiceover:** Van Ness Media knows that parents and schools don't really want kids exposed to advertising. So they don't allow any advertising in their software. This is a major selling point for their company, and CEO Maria Van Ness mentions it in interviews all the time.
Clip of Maria Van Ness on CNN	**MARIA VAN NESS:** Van Ness Media products are proudly free of advertising. We aim to make money by selling software, not our customers' attention spans. That's important to schools, and rightfully so. Our commitment to having zero advertising within our products sets us apart, and it's helped us grow.

Anchor with Corey Fox	**ANC:** Let's say certain software doesn't have any advertising in it. Like, its users don't see any ads while they're using it. Does that mean any information the users put into that software is private, and it won't be used for advertising? **COREY FOX:** No, not necessarily. The company that makes the software might still be collecting information about its users and building detailed profiles about them. If the company gives or sells those profiles to someone else, the users might see targeted advertising on a different website, or in a different app.
Anchor on Camera	**ANC:** Van Ness Media doesn't allow anyone to advertise to their users *inside* their software. But could they be giving away their users' personal information for advertising in *other* places? In order to find out, *The Underground News* decided to do a test. We created a fake person named Jacob Brown, and we signed him up for a Van Ness Media account.

Anchor in Brielle's Room	**ANC:** We're creating our fake Van Ness Media account on this laptop. It was completely reformatted, so there's no personal information on it. In order to make sure ads aren't targeted using old searches, we're using a new browser that's never been used on this computer. As an extra precaution, we cleared the cookies. Here's the welcome screen: New users click here. It's a good thing they offer new users a one-week free trial. We don't have much of a budget here at *The Underground News*. All set. Twelve-year-old Jacob Brown is ready to use the full suite of Van Ness Media software.
Planet Pizza Newsletter	**ANC voiceover:** We decided to give our fake user some very specific interests: space and pizza. We filled his Van Ness Media account with information about those two things and only those two things. We were careful not to put information about him anywhere else on the internet, so that advertisers could *only* get this information from Van Ness Media. They claim that they care about their users' privacy. But will Van Ness Media actually keep Jacob Brown's information private?

Anchor on Camera	**ANC on camera:** One day has passed, and it's time to check Jacob Brown's email account.
Laptop on Screen	**ANC voiceover:** Remember his interests, which *only* Van Ness Media could know? Look at the ads that appeared in his email inbox the very next day. Domino's Pizza, Pizza Hut, and the planetarium.
Anchor on Camera	**ANC:** This is Ashley Simon-Hockheimer with proof that nothing you do in Van Ness Media software is private.
Anchor in Inner Harbor	**ANC:** We decided to talk to some kids to see how they feel about the idea of their personal information being shared with advertisers without their knowledge.
Anchor with Boy #1	**ANC:** Do you use Van Ness Media at school? **BOY 1:** Oh yeah. I'm working on a presentation about the American West. **ANC:** Who do you think can see what you put in that presentation? **BOY 1:** Um. Just me? Unless I show it to my parents or something so they can help. And my teacher too, but not till I'm done. **ANC:** What if I told you that Van Ness Media was taking all the information you put in that project and giving it to outside companies so they can show you ads. And maybe making money from it. And if you open their apps on your phone, they are keeping track of your location. **BOY 1:** Um. I don't know. That'd be kind of weird.

Girl #1 in Harbor	**GIRL 1:** Like, they're looking at my home-work? And they know where I go in real life?
Teenager #1 in Harbor	**TEENAGER 1:** I don't really care. I mean, it's not like my art project is top secret. I don't have anything to hide.
Girl #2 in Harbor	**GIRL 2:** That's creepy. I'd definitely think more about what I put in there, if I know someone else is seeing it. And why's it their business where I go?
Boy #2 in Harbor	**BOY 2:** You mean someone's paying money to read my book report? Why aren't I getting that money, if I wrote the thing?
Mom in Harbor	**MOM:** I would not be happy about that. The school is supposed to keep our kids' information private. These are children we're talking about.
Grandma in Harbor	**GRANDMA:** No, no, no. I don't think schools would allow that. They can't use photos of children for as little as a school newsletter without parents signing a permission slip. So they wouldn't let my grandbabies' work and location be shared with just anyone. Not without letting us know and asking permission.
Anchor on Camera	**ANC:** She raised a good point about permission. In order to use Van Ness Media, our fake user, Jacob Brown, had to have a parent or guardian agree to the terms and conditions and the privacy policy. But what, exactly, was he agreeing to?

Privacy Policy	**ANC voiceover:** "In respect of processing of Personal Data detailed in this Privacy Policy, such processing is necessary for the purposes of a legitimate interest pursued by Van Ness Media, and we have assessed that such interests are not overridden by the interests or fundamental rights and freedoms of the persons to whom the Personal Data relates."
Anchor on Camera	**ANC:** Huh?
Corey Fox in Office	**COREY FOX:** Yes, we all agree to terms of service, and websites have to share their privacy policies. But does anyone read them, let alone understand what they're agreeing to? These documents are dozens of pages long, with tiny print, and filled with complicated legal jargon. We're often signing away all our rights, without even knowing it.
Anchor with Corey Fox	**ANC:** If it's software kids use at school, who agrees to the terms and reviews the privacy policy? **COREY FOX:** Whoever approves the use of the software in the school. If a certain software company has a contract with a school system, someone from the school or the district would most likely grant permission on behalf of all the students.

Anchor on Camera	**ANC:** I asked the principal of my school who agreed to the terms and conditions. It wasn't him, and he didn't know who it was, because all of Baltimore City Public Schools has a contract with Van Ness Media. *The Underground News* tried to talk to someone at the district headquarters, but no one returned our phone calls or emails. So, we still don't know who's granting permission for Van Ness Media to access Baltimore City Public Schools' students' personal information and creations. But we do know one thing: Van Ness Media is hungry for more.
Maria Van Ness Announcement	**MARIA VAN NESS:** I am excited to announce the newest addition to the Van Ness Media suite of products: Van Ness Dream Journal. This is an app for brainstorming, daydreaming, and doodling. A place for ideas that are still germinating, and not yet ready to be shared.
Anchor on Camera	**ANC:** Not yet ready to be shared. Except that Van Ness Media is able to share it with anyone they want. We asked Van Ness Media about that very question. Their response?

Email from Van Ness Media Public Relations	**ANC voiceover:** "Van Ness Media proudly offers advertising-free software for educational use. The full details of our user agreement and privacy policy are available on our website." They're referring to the same long, wordy agreement we looked at before. The one no one at my school knew anything about or personally agreed to.
Anchor with Corey Fox	**ANC:** What about people who say they don't really care about their digital fingerprints? That they have nothing to hide? **COREY FOX:** There are trade-offs, right? Because we certainly get things out of the deal. Directions, discounts, relevant information. But most people don't really understand what they're giving away in exchange. That there are companies out there that know more about you than you may know yourself. It's one thing if it's just used for advertising, okay, to manipulate you into buying something. But what if the information is used in a different way? What if companies try to make you vote for a particular person, or not vote at all? What if you can't get health insurance because you once did some internet searches about cancer? What if you're arrested because you were in a certain place around the time a crime occurred?

Anchor with Corey Fox cont.	You may think you don't need privacy if you have nothing to hide, but there's a reason companies compile and pay big money for information about all of us. They wouldn't do it if it weren't valuable.
Anchor on Camera	**ANC:** What if companies use it to try and stop users from doing things they don't like? When *The Underground News* started working on this story, we were editing it in Van Ness Movie Maker. That meant Van Ness Media knew everything we were putting in our report.
Error Message on Screen	**ANC voiceover:** And suddenly, every member of our team got locked out of the software with an error message like this. Here's our own video editor talking about it.
Brielle by her Computer	**BRIELLE:** According to Van Ness Media, we were kicked out because we violated the terms of service. They set the rules, and I guess the rules say their business gets to stay private? So I finished editing this episode using Final Cut Pro, and it's so much better than Van Ness Movie Maker!
Anchor on Camera	**ANC:** Van Ness Media claims to care about its users' privacy. Here's a clip of Maria Van Ness being interviewed on CNN just last month.

Maria Van Ness on CNN	**MARIA VAN NESS:** We *are* targeting the education market—kids ages three through eighteen—which means we have an extra responsibility to protect our users. Sure, there's free software available. But it's not really free. It's being paid for by advertising, which means users are being constantly bombarded by ads, whether they realize it or not. And not realizing it is when it's most harmful, especially to children.
Anchor on Camera	**ANC:** But here's what Maria Van Ness had to say when I confronted her about this myself.
Maria Van Ness in Federal Hill Park	**MARIA VAN NESS:** Developing brains are very impressionable. That's why they're so valuable to advertisers.
	I thought I'd stay out of the whole thing, but I couldn't let such a valuable opportunity go to waste.
	ANC: You're lying to people. And you're trying to stop us from telling the truth. The three of us—we all just got locked out of our Van Ness Media accounts for violating the terms of service.
	MARIA VAN NESS: I'm not lying to anyone. If you three were using Movie Maker, you agreed to the terms, and to the privacy policy. Not just you, but hundreds of thousands of users, all over the country. It's all written down for everyone to see.

Maria Van Ness in Federal Hill Park cont.	**MARIA VAN NESS:** I make the best digital media software for the education market, hands down. Surely, you agree? I'd like to see you make your little show with a different editing program. Kids use my creations to make things like—what is it?—*The Undercover News.* And I use *their* creations to fund the operation and grow the company. Everyone wins. **ANC:** But . . . **MARIA VAN NESS:** But what? Privacy? No one cares about privacy. Not if you give them a good product in exchange. Some people think they care, but not enough to do anything about it. Right?
Anchor on Camera	**ANC:** I guess we'll just have to wait and see. I'm Ashley Simon-Hockheimer with the Renegade Reporters, and this is *The Underground News.*

CHAPTER 33

Community Reacts to News

Once *The Underground News* episode wrapped up, *The News at Nine* anchors were back on the screen, looking serious and somber. "Thank you to *The Underground News* team for that important report. I'm Damion Skinner."

"I'm Harry E. Levin. This has been *The News at Nine*, brought to you by Baltimore-based Van Ness Media."

When the show ended, everyone in Mr. Brooks's classroom, including Mr. Brooks, looked at Ash, stunned. Some of them applauded. But Ash didn't feel proud or embarrassed or anything, really. It was like she wasn't a person, but a piece of furniture, lifelessly taking in what was going on around her.

When Harry and Damion arrived, Mr. Brooks led everyone in a discussion about the report. Kids had a lot to say. And not just in their class. Other teachers talked about it with their classes too. Kids talked about it during lunch and recess, then went home and talked about it with their families. Parents logged onto the school's online portal, or to

The Underground News YouTube channel, and watched the episode themselves. Many of them called Mr. Carver and demanded answers. Mr. Carver called the district headquarters and demanded answers. The superintendent sent an email to parents with a bland statement from Van Ness Media, everyone assuring one another that they'd look into what was going on.

They weren't the only ones who planned to look into it. On Wednesday night, Ash's dads received an email.

Dear Mr. Simon and Mr. Hockheimer,

My name is Tenley Nay, and I'm a reporter for *The Baltimore Sun.* My son is in third grade at John Dos Passos, and I got your contact info from the school portal.

I watched your daughter's excellent report on Van Ness Media. It was investigative journalism at its finest! I'm digging a bit more and writing a story for the *Sun.* I'd love to interview Ashley, with your permission, of course. Please call or email me asap.

T.N.

Ash replied herself. She knew exactly what she wanted to say.

Dear Ms. Nay,

My dads gave permission for me to do the interview. I didn't investigate the story by myself, though. I had lots of help from Maya Joshi-Zachariah and Brielle Diamond. Harry E. Levin and Ms. Sullivan helped me put it on *The News at Nine.* I hope we can help with your article.

Sincerely,
ASH

CHAPTER 34

Regional Newspaper Amplifies Story

On Saturday evening, Dad, Abba, and Sadie all came running into the bathroom while Ash was giving Beckett his bath. "Breaking news alert from *The Baltimore Sun*!" Dad announced, holding out his phone.

Ash gasped. She dried her hands on a towel and took Dad's phone to read the notification aloud. "'Breaking news: Sixth-grade journalists expose Van Ness Media software for secretly storing, selling kids' personal information.'"

"That's you!" Sadie screeched. "*You're* the sixth-grade journalists! And they're storing and selling *my* personal information!"

"I wouldn't be so excited about that second part, Sadie," Abba said with a chuckle.

"I don't care," Sadie shouted. "We're famous!"

"Fay-us!" shouted Beckett, splashing water everywhere.

Ash clicked on the alert to bring up the story. Her own reporting was in *The Baltimore Sun*. She scrolled down to see how long the article was. It was long. There was a picture of her with Maya and Brielle, taken by a photographer that the *Sun* had sent over to her house yesterday. There were two images from episodes of *The Underground News*, one with the logo Maya had drawn and one with Ash in their basement studio. There was a shot of Harry and Damion in *The News at Nine* studio, and one of the Van Ness Media building in Harbor East. The last photo was from the footage of Maria Van Ness in Federal Hill Park, the CEO standing on the hill with her headquarters in the background.

Dad offered to finish bathing Beckett so that Ash could read the article in its entirety. She planted herself on the floor outside the bathroom and read it twice. Tenley Nay's reporting was thorough and incriminating, exposing the names of the data brokers with which Van Ness Media partnered. She talked about the possibility of Van Ness Media having violated something called COPPA, which stood for the Children's Online Privacy Protection Act. Ms. Nay didn't just write about Maria Van Ness and her shady practices. She wrote about Ash and Maya and Brielle and how they'd uncovered what was going on at Van Ness Media first.

Inside the bathroom, Sadie was shouting and Beckett was splashing. Downstairs, Abba was reading the article on the computer and texting grandparents. Ash sat and breathed, a bubble of pride filling her chest.

Dad poked his head into the hallway. "Did they get everything right?"

"Yeah," Ash said. "For the most part."

"Maria Van Ness thought no one would listen to you, huh? You certainly proved her wrong about that."

"Thanks, Dad." The balloon in Ash's chest swelled even bigger. But then it started to deflate, ever so slightly. It was one thing to make people aware of what Van Ness Media was doing. It was another to know that they were going to stop.

"She also said nobody would care," Ash said to Dad.

He kissed the top of Ash's head. "I have a feeling she'll be wrong about that too. We'll just have to wait and see."

They didn't have to wait long.

Just two days later, while she and Maya were waiting to cross Light Street on their way home from school, Ash got a phone call from a number that looked familiar.

"Hi, Ash, it's Tenley Nay from *The Baltimore Sun*."

Ash looked at Maya. "Tenley Nay!" she mouthed.

"Holy moly," Maya whispered.

Ash stuck a finger in her left ear and pressed her phone closer to her right. "Hi," she said.

"Listen," said Ms. Nay. "I just got word from my contact at North Avenue that Baltimore City Public Schools is ending its contract with Van Ness Media, effective immediately. They may renew the agreement eventually, but only if Van

Ness Media agrees to stop tracking and selling its users' personal information."

Ash stopped walking. "For real?"

"For real. They're going to send out an email to all the families in the district tomorrow. I'm going to get a story in tomorrow's paper, and I know everyone up on TV Hill is going to jump on it too. But since you and your team are to thank for this development, I thought it was only fair that *The Underground News* break it first."

Ash stood on the street corner, warm amazement edging out the cold November air.

"So, what do you think?" Ms. Nay asked. "Can you and Maya and Brielle act fast?"

Ash was in too much shock to respond. A real, grown-up reporter was offering to let her break a real news story before anyone else. She stood frozen on the corner until an ambulance passed by, sirens blaring, and jolted her back to reality. "Yes," she replied. "We'll do it."

"Great," Ms. Nay said. "I'm going to text you the number for my contact at City Schools. She's waiting for your call. I've got to get my story in print and online tomorrow, so you've got until tonight if you want to break it first."

"Okay," Ash said, starting a mental list of all the things she and her friends would have to do to get their episode out so quickly. "I'm on it."

Maya tugged on Ash's arm and stared at her expectantly.

"Can I give your number to some local TV anchors too?" Ms. Nay asked. "Check with your dads."

"Um, sure. I'll check."

"Oh! Keep an eye on your email. I'm expecting confirmation of some other news any minute now. From a contact at the Environmental Control Board."

Ash had no clue what that meant, but she could tell Ms. Nay was smiling when she said it.

"Send me the link to your episode when it's live."

"Okay," Ash said again, her head spinning.

"Great. Let's get to work." Ms. Nay paused long enough for Ash to think she'd hung up, only she was still in too much shock to move the phone from her ear. That was good, because the *Sun* reporter had one last thing to say: "And Ashley? Congratulations."

THE UNDERGROUND NEWS, EPISODE 5

REPORTER: Ashley Simon-Hockheimer
VIDEOGRAPHER: Maya Joshi-Zachariah
EDITOR: Brielle Diamond
STORY SCOUT: Sadie Simon-Hockheimer
SLUG: Canceled contract

VIDEO	AUDIO
Anchor on Camera	**ANC:** Breaking news: Baltimore City Schools has canceled its contract with Van Ness Media, effective immediately. I'm Ashley Simon-Hockheimer with the Renegade Reporters, and you're watching *The Underground News*.
Intro and Credits	NONE
Anchor on Camera	**ANC:** About two weeks ago, *The Underground News* reported that Van Ness Media, the fastest-growing educational software company in the United States, has been keeping detailed profiles on all of its school-age users and selling that information to advertisers.

| Anchor on Camera cont. | **ANC:** CEO Maria Van Ness confessed that to me, Ashley Simon-Hockheimer, and with the help of anchor Harry E. Levin, we aired that confession on my school's news show, *The News at Nine*. That led to an article in *The Baltimore Sun* and other news media. As more people became aware of what Van Ness Media was doing, they began to call their schools and ask that something change.

I am now able to report that Baltimore City Public Schools has canceled its contract with Van Ness Media, effective immediately. Here with more is Head of Technology for Baltimore City Schools, Jennifer Bishop. |
| --- | --- |
| Jennifer Bishop in Office | **JENNIFER BISHOP:** The safety and privacy of our students is of the utmost importance. For that reason, we are putting a hold on the use of all Van Ness Media products in all of our classrooms, effective immediately. It's unfortunate, because Van Ness Media makes good software that teaches important twenty-first-century skills. But storing and selling our students' personal details and locations for marketing purposes is unacceptable, especially when one of the reasons we selected this software in the first place is that it claimed to be free of advertising. |

Anchor with Jennifer Bishop in Office	**ANC:** Were you aware of the terms of service and privacy policy with Van Ness Media? **JENNIFER BISHOP:** I'll leave that question for our legal department. But I will say this: Now that we know what's going on, we are not going to stand for it. It's our job to educate the children of Baltimore City, but we're also responsible for their safety while they're in school, and that includes their safety online. **ANC:** Do you think you might allow students to use Van Ness Media software in the future? **JENNIFER BISHOP:** We are willing to consider it, but only if Van Ness Media is willing to change their privacy policy and terms of service to guarantee they will not track, store, save, share, or sell any personal information about our users.

Anchor on Camera	**ANC:** We are already getting word that schools in surrounding counties are ending their contracts as well. Subscribe to this channel for more updates on this developing story and other important news from the best sixth-grade journalists in Baltimore City. Before we sign off, we have one more piece of breaking news about the Van Ness Media CEO, Maria Van Ness. This news is straight from the Baltimore City Environmental Control Board, and here to report it is *The Underground News* Story Scout, my sister, Sadie.
Sadie in Studio	**SADIE:** Hi, I'm Sadie Simon-Hockheimer. Thanks to video evidence from this show, the "dog poo bandit" has finally been caught.
Image of Citation	**SADIE voiceover:** Federal Hill resident Maria Van Ness has been issued a three-hundred-dollar citation for failing to pick up after her pet.
Sadie in Studio	**SADIE:** Remember, folks, it's a crime to not scoop your pet's poop!
Anchor on Camera	**ANC:** I'm Ashley Simon-Hockheimer with the Renegade Reporters, and you're watching *The Underground News*.

CHAPTER 35

LIVE: Ash on Air

It was a real scramble for the *Underground News* team to get the episode filmed, edited, parent-approved, and live by the end of the day. Since it was a Friday and Brielle was in charge of the last part of the process, her parents agreed to have the Renegade Reporters spend the night at their house. The three girls had big plans for their impromptu sleepover, but by the time they hit the upload button on the completed episode, it was nearly midnight, and it took all their fading energy to crawl into their sleeping bags and say good night.

They didn't wake up until ten the next morning. When they went downstairs, Brielle's parents and grandfather greeted them with waffles, hot chocolate, and three paper copies of *The Baltimore Sun*, where the news of Van Ness Media's canceled contract was on the front page. "It's official, girls," her granddad said, raising his coffee mug for a toast. "You made something happen."

When Abba came to pick up Ash and Maya at eleven, he

was carrying a list of names and phone numbers. "WYPR wants you for a radio interview sometime today. While you're in the studio, they said you can also record a segment for tomorrow morning's *Weekend Edition,* which broadcasts nationally."

Brielle's eyes bugged out. "Nationally?"

"Yep," said Abba. "On stations all over the country."

Ash's waffle did a backflip in her stomach. She was going to be on NPR!

"You got a TV request too," Abba continued. "WJZ wants to interview the whole team on the five o'clock news."

Maya, who'd been squeezing her friends' hands tighter with the mention of each media outlet, limply let go.

"You should do it, Brielle," her mom said.

Brielle looked like her mom had said she should tap-dance with a banana on her head. "Did you *see* my five seconds on *The Underground News*? My face? My voice? I'm going to stay behind the camera for the rest of my life."

"But we'll get to be on the real news!" Ash said. "It's a dream come true."

"*Your* dream come true," Brielle corrected. "But it would be cool to see their studio, with all the equipment. Maya gets it. Right, Maya?"

But to everyone's surprise, Maya gave the slightest of shrugs and said, quietly but clearly, "I'll do the interview."

Ash stared at her best friend, the same girl who used to

be too shy to order her own food at a restaurant. "Amazing!" Ash said, throwing her arms around her and jumping up and down. "You're going to be awesome!"

And so, at five o'clock, the Renegade Reports found themselves in a real TV studio. The cameraman showed Maya his setup. Brielle got a tour of the control booth. And Ash sat, for the first time, behind a real anchor's desk. She basked in the lights, the cameras, the action.

"Nervous?" the WJZ anchor asked.

"Kind of," Ash admitted. "I'm more used to *asking* the questions."

"I know," the anchor said, straightening his tie. "And don't stop. You've got a big career ahead of you."

For real? Ash thought. But there was no time to ask. Maya was escorted to the chair next to hers. The director began counting down. The cameraman got into position. And the anchors cleared their throats, ready to roll.

CHAPTER 36

11/11 Brings Endings, Beginnings

It was a whirlwind weekend. The news and radio segments led to calls from reporters at the *Washington Post* and the *New York Times*. Van Ness Media's secretive selling of children's private data made headlines all over the country, as did the team of young reporters who'd originally broken the story. *The Underground News* got more and more subscribers. Ash had a feeling that this was just the beginning, and it was the beginning of something big.

For the second time in less than a year, Ash and Maya found themselves with a viral video. This one was the raw footage of Maria Van Ness in Federal Hill Park. It racked up 2.5 million views in one week. They added a link to the full *Underground News* episode about Van Ness Media, and close to one million people watched that as well. They got lots of emails from people who'd seen their report, but the best one of all was from the admissions office at Baltimore School for the Arts, saying they hoped Brielle would apply to their filmmaking program for next year.

For every step Ash took into the spotlight, Maria Van Ness tried to step out of it. She refused to give interviews, leaving a spokesman to comment on her behalf, usually with the same vague talking points about there being no advertising in Van Ness Media software. When reporters pressed him about the claim that they were still selling their users' details to advertisers, the spokesman never had a convincing response.

Maria Van Ness was lying low in another way too. Ash and Sadie didn't have to dodge a single pile of dog poo on their walk to school Monday morning.

But Ash wondered if Harry had stepped in some. She found him on a bench outside the entrance to John Dos Passos Elementary, his backpack in his lap and a scowl on his face. His eyes lasered in on Ash as she approached. She said goodbye to her sister and walked slowly up to the bench.

"Well, you finally got what you wanted," Harry said. "I'm no longer lead anchor of *The News at Nine*."

Ash's mouth dropped open. "What? Why not?"

"Because there *is* no more *News at Nine*. We lost our sponsor. They're taking back all their equipment. The show is canceled, effective immediately."

Ash slowly lowered herself onto the bench next to Harry. Had there really been a time when this was what she'd wanted? Yes, back in the beginning of the year.

She'd been so bitter, so jealous, that she'd have taken a wicked pleasure in *The News at Nine* being canceled. *Schadenfreude,* she remembered Olive calling it. *Taking pleasure in someone else's pain.* But she didn't feel that way anymore, partly because she'd had her own show to focus on, but also because Harry had become a good anchor. Great, even.

"I can't believe this happened today," Harry said glumly, "of all days."

"What do you mean?" Ash asked.

"It's November eleventh," he explained in a voice that suggested it should have been common sense. "Eleven-eleven, and I'm eleven."

"Uh-huh," Ash said in a voice that conveyed just how strange she thought Harry was being. "I'm eleven too."

"But I'm Harry *E. Levin*," Harry said. "This is my day. In the only year I'll be eleven. I knew something big would happen. I just thought it'd be big in a good way. And that it'd happen at eleven eleven this morning, or maybe tonight."

Oh, Ash thought. That was kind of cool. It was also terrible. His show was canceled on the day he'd been looking forward to for eleven years. And it wasn't his fault. Harry had helped Ash report the truth when Van Ness Media had tried to silence her. They couldn't silence Ash, but they could silence Harry, and they did.

"I'm sorry," Ash said genuinely. "I never thought about what my report might mean for *The News at Nine*."

"I did," Harry said. "I mean, I figured they'd cancel it if we aired your story."

"You did?" Ash shifted to look right at him. "And you decided to do it anyway?"

"Well, yeah," Harry said, fiddling with his shark-tooth necklace. "I mean, it was important news. And good reporting." He held her gaze for a second, then looked down at his backpack.

Ash had been complimented on her reporting by print journalists, radio broadcasters, even professional TV news anchors. But it was this compliment from Harry E. Levin that made her bones feel like jelly. "Your reporting's good too," she said. "I'm going to really miss watching *The News at Nine*."

"Liar," Harry said.

"For real!" Ash said, getting annoyed. But then she saw that he was smiling. She hit him with her elbow and smiled back. "I'm serious. You're a good anchor. Not as good as I am, but you're getting there."

"Yeah, yeah," Harry said, rolling his eyes.

The two of them got up, put on their backpacks, and started walking to class. As they passed the dark *News at Nine* studio, Ash had an idea. She probably should have saved it for 11:11 a.m., but it'd be too hard to wait. "Hey, do you want to join *The Underground News*? I'd have to ask Maya and Brielle, but I'm sure they'd be okay with adding a co-anchor."

Harry stopped. "You're seriously asking if I want to be a 'renegade reporter'?"

Ash shrugged. "If you can't beat 'em, join 'em."

Harry crossed his arms. "Who says I can't beat 'em?"

"Um," Ash said. "We've got, like, a hundred thousand subscribers."

"Whatever," Harry said, his face transforming into a familiar smirk. "Just one big story, and my friends and I will have twice that."

Ash looked at her rival and genuinely hoped he was right. "You know what?" she said. "May the best anchor win."

AUTHOR'S NOTE

Van Ness Media does not exist in real life, but digital tracking does. Every time you and I use our phones, computers, or other devices connected to the internet, we leave a digital fingerprint. Companies collect and store that information, creating detailed profiles of who we are, where we go, and what we do. They use that data to show us targeted advertisements, recommendations, search results, and more. When we agree to various privacy policies and terms of service, we're often granting permission for companies to use our personal information any way they'd like, which might include sharing it with other companies or selling it to data brokers. There are laws aimed at protecting the digital privacy of children under the age of thirteen, but there are also numerous instances of companies breaking those laws.

You can do a few things to limit tracking on your phone and in your browser, but it's impossible to avoid being tracked entirely. Whether this makes you as uneasy as it does Maya or you're as indifferent as Brielle, it's important to be aware that it's happening, especially as more and more of everyday life moves online. A good source for more information is *Eyes and Spies: How You're Tracked and Why You Should Know* by Tanya Lloyd Kyi.

If you care deeply about digital privacy—or any cause!—remember that, like Ash and her friends, you have the power to use your voice for positive change.

While I'm distinguishing between fact and fiction in *The Renegade Reporters,* I'll note that Ash's neighborhood in Baltimore is real, but John Dos Passos Elementary is not. If Ash and her friends attended a real Baltimore City public school, they'd have graduated elementary school in fifth grade, and Brielle would have to wait a few more years before applying to the Baltimore School for the Arts, since their film program begins in ninth grade.

A real dog poo bandit was on the loose in Federal Hill some years ago, and a scooter (not a bike) was really stolen from and returned to Riverside Park (believe it!). As far as I'm aware, both culprits remain at large.

ACKNOWLEDGMENTS

When I do school visits, kids often ask me where I get the ideas for my books. Well, I got the idea for this book from doing school visits!

When I was in elementary school, sixth graders took turns reading the morning announcements over the loudspeaker in the main office. But visiting schools as an author, I discovered that there are a surprising number of schools in America—both private and public—where the morning announcements now take the form of a television show. Schools have professional-quality studios, with microphones and green screens and advanced editing equipment. The kids do everything, from pitching and writing stories to holding cue cards and cameras to reporting and directing the finished product. As a visiting author, I've had the honor of being a guest on a number of school TV shows, and the students running them—broadcasting experts all—inspired me to write a book about kids who work on a show like this. I owe a big thank-you to the

2016 news crews at Sunset Palms Elementary and Timber Trace Elementary in Florida for sparking the initial idea. And I'm especially grateful to the "National Pickles" at Tuckahoe Elementary in Virginia, who generously showed me the inner workings of their News @ 9 and even inspired the name for the show in this book.

My research on digital privacy was broad, but I owe many thanks to the Center for Humane Technology, the *New York Times* Privacy Project, and the contributors to both.

A million thanks to the brilliant Swapna Haddow, Corinne Brinkley, Amy Roza, and Matt Freeman for their thoughtful feedback on the many characters in this book whose lived experience would be different from my own. The always supportive Shawn K. Stout, Elisabeth Dahl, Erin Hagar, and Lori Steel gave me early encouragement, guidance, and cake! Thanks, as always, to Flip Brophy and Nell Pierce for helping my words reach the wider world. I am lucky and grateful to have you both on my side. The same goes for the team at Dial, especially my editor, Dana Chidiac, who asked the right questions, helped me find the right answers, and cheered nonstop along the way.

Finally, lots of love to Federal Hill Preparatory School #45 and to Baltimore City, places I am proud to have called home. I strove to capture the vibrancy of these communities in this book, but there's nothing like the real thing.